LETTING GO:

Emily's Homecoming

By: Lisa A. Tippette

DEDICATION

This book is first and foremost dedicated to God, whose incredible love, power and strength enabled me to let go of the expectations of others, endowed me with the creativity and talent to write, and gave me the freedom to be who He created me to be.

And to Robbie, my amazing husband, who taught me to let go of the hurts of the past and the worries of tomorrow, and live for the simple pleasures of the present. You'll never know how much you have influenced and changed my life!
I love you, sweetheart!

Finally, to Moma and Daddy, who have held my hand and my heart since I was a little girl, never letting go, always guiding and supporting me down every path I have traveled. Your constant love, guidance, and support have helped to shape and mold me into the person I am today.
I love your both dearly!

LETTING GO:

Emily's Homecoming

CHAPTER 1

*T*he smoldering fire hissed and crackled as Brian heaped two more pieces of dry, seasoned oak to the searing pile of partially burnt wood. The flames instantly leapt up, dancing and licking wildly into an empty vacuum of space and time. When its showy display was over, the flames quickly died down, joining the heaping company of glowing ashes beneath it. He repeated the toilsome task, hoping to resuscitate any lingering sparks into a warm and roaring blaze, patiently forgiving the stubbornness of the wood to cooperate and bring forth new life. New life. He thought about Emily and the irony of the situation, comparing it to the glowing embers in front of him, which singed and ignited the fresh wood he fed it. Likewise, the analogy burned and stung at his own heart.

The heat from the newly birthed flames warmed and reddened his face, and tiny reflections of flames flickered in the translucent teardrops that had now filled his eyes. He grabbed some thin pieces of kindling and snapped them into with his bear hands. A stray splinter lodged itself deeply in a crevice in his right palm. He quickly thrust the broken sticks in the fire and grabbed his injured hand. "Ouch!" he hollered, quickly plucking the foreign object from his throbbing palm. It seemed pain was a constant companion these days; his only companion, in fact, since Emily had left.

But that was her decision. They could have made it work. He was certain of it. She just lacked faith. Faith in him, and in herself. And most of all, faith in God. In fact, she blamed God.

"How could He have let this happen?" she bitterly asked repeatedly, not willing to accept that *"rain falls on the just, as well as the unjust."*

"That's where your faith comes in -that's when you need God the most", he would remind her time and again.

"I don't need a God that punishes me, while all those other sorry whores have two and three kids, and have never even stepped foot inside a church! What kind of justice is that?" she screamed out belligerently, in hollow pain.

Emily was just a new babe in Christ. Her faith had barely taken root. It really WAS a huge first test of faith; one she obviously was not prepared for. And one she failed miserably. Brian couldn't really blame her. Even old Job in the Bible had lived a full life before God allowed Satan to take it all away. Emily was still a young woman. It was her first child. THEIR first child. Maybe God did ask a little too much, too soon.

Brian had his own questions, as well. Why wait until she was eight months along? Why not just take it before it was even a few weeks old? In fact, why give it to her AT ALL if He was just going to take it later? Like the blazing fire before him, the questions burned deep holes in his mind – and his heart. But the answers never came. Even so, his faith was a little stronger. He had learned over the years not to question God, only to trust Him. He knew the enemy would use questions to breed doubt, and doubt would lead to temptation, temptation to sin.

He tried desperately to console Emily, hoping his faith would sustain them both. But she would have no part of it. She spit defiantly in the face of faith, tossing it out like a used paper cup. Being in such deep emotional pain, she was ripe for the picking, and Satan had no problem in winning her over. At least for the time being anyway. Brian was all too familiar with the enemy's cunning deceptions and scheming trickery to fool Christians into turning against God. He had been an easy victim a few times, himself, saved only by the grace of a loving, merciful, and forgiving God who graciously guided him back into the fold. Emily, too, was a Christian, and even though she had strayed off course, he still believed God would lead her back home, too. One day, Emily WOULD come home.

He glanced up at the old antique clock on the mantle. Eleven-thirty. It had been almost a month since she left and at least that long since he'd had a decent night's sleep. In fact, the nights and days seem to run blindly into each other since he had been laid off from his job at the local glass factory, and had no call to get up in the mornings. And with Emily down for the count, it was obvious the enemy was now coming after him. In fact, now Brian was the one feeling a little like ole' Job. No wife, no children, no job. How much longer would it be before, like Job, he lost it all?

"NO!" he yelled out to his faceless enemy. "You will NOT get me, too, Satan! In the name of, and by the blood of Jesus, I command you to leave me alone!" He dropped to his knees, lifted his weary heart to the heavens, and begged God for strength to fight the battles he weakly faced. He prayed for deliverance from evil. He prayed for restoration of his marriage. He prayed for guidance. He prayed for forgiveness. He prayed for peace. Most of all, he prayed for Emily. Cleansing tears flooded his eyes and formed cylindrical puddles as they fell to the hardwood floor around him. He stayed hunched over on the floor for what seemed like hours, crying his heart and soul out to the only One who understood his pain.

Suddenly, he felt a calming peace gently swathe over him like a warm, protective blanket. His weary loins filled with Sampson-like strength, enabling him to lift himself off the floor. He looked up and out the front window. Brilliant moonlight streamed in and lit up the whole room with the magnificent glory of Almighty God! Once again, God's grace met him at his level of faith, even if it was lying almost supine on the floor. God would have done the same for Emily. If only she had just a mustard seed's worth of faith, He would have given her the strength to make it through losing baby Jacob. But all she had was anger. Bitterness. Loss. Empty arms. Weak faith was no competition with brutal enemies such as these.

Brian rubbed his bleary, bloodshot eyes, and then

collapsed back on the mahogany red leather couch behind him, one leg still straddling the floor. He punched the stiff pillow behind his head with what little strength he had left, then tossed the handmade woven quilt from the back of the couch over his weary body, still fully dressed, with the exception of his Durango boots, which he had shed earlier after bringing in the last load of firewood. He prayed sleep would take over where exhaustion left off. For weeks, he had been keeping vigil from the couch since Emily left; their cold, empty bed haunting him like a lifeless ghost. Winters were cold and lonely enough in the mountains without sleeping alone in a king sized bed, filled with king sized memories of happier times. Besides, she could come back at any time of the day or night. It's what he had prayed so fervently for every night, and his faith in God assured him she would be back. Consequently, he wanted to be right there waiting, when she walked in that front door.

How he longed to wrap his brawny arms around her petite frame, draw her into his manly chest and enshroud her body and heart with his love. How he wanted to feel the silky softness of her long, auburn hair against his face; inhale the angelic scent of her meadow sweet perfume. How he wanted to dance playfully around the room with her. Like they used to before - before things got serious and complicated. Most of all, how he wanted to fix her broken heart - like he fixed the mower, and the loose board on the porch, and the broken mirror in the bathroom. He had fixed so many things since they bought that little rustic cabin in the Silver Ridge Mountains. He was a born handyman. All he needed was the right tools. But now, for the first time in his life, there was something he couldn't fix. Something he didn't know HOW to fix. And the only tool he had was his faith. Would it do the job? Would it be enough to fix Emily? Would it be enough to bring her home?

With sleep finally bearing down on his swollen, smoke and tear laden eyes, he relinquished his body, mind and being to a dull state of unconsciousness. A few fading embers crackled one last time in the dying fire. A dim nightlight glowed on the front porch. For Emily. For when she came back. And he knew she would be back. One day she WOULD come home!

CHAPTER 2

Tap, tap. Tap, tap, tap. Brian groggily roused to a light, and annoying tapping at the door. The sun was just barely squinting in through the half-drawn plantation shutters, but it was just enough daylight to pry open his sleepy eyes. *Tap, tap, tap.* Body and mind finally connected as he came to an upright position. The quilt that had warmed him through the night fell to the floor. He picked it up and tossed it behind him to its home on the back of the couch. *Tap, tap, tap.* The persistent visitor knocked again.

"Alright, alright, I'm coming!" he grumbled under his breath, dragging his size eleven feet to the front door. He peered through the peephole, hoping against all hope it might be Emily on the other side. Once again, disappointment won out. He unlatched the deadbolt and swung open the heavy, rustic cabin door.

"What took you so long?" she asked, marching right past him, carrying a dishtowel-covered pan.

"Sorry, Ma, I was still asleep. Guess I didn't get to bed 'til late last night."

"Well, I'm sorry to wake you so early, son, but I just took these blueberry muffins from the oven and thought you might like a hot one for breakfast. Sit down and I'll fix you some coffee to go with 'em."

Brian's step mom, Pauline, lived in the detached in-law quarters behind his cabin. It was a smaller version of his own full-size cabin, and in fact, the reason he and Emily bought the cabin in the first place. Before his father died from a fatal heart attack six years earlier, he had promised him that he would always look after Pauline, who was more than just a step mom - she was the ONLY mom Brian had ever known. He never even knew his biological mother, as she died in childbirth, after giving birth to him. His father, Jesse, married Pauline about a year later, and she took right to being a wife and a mother. They never had any other children, and it was many years later before Brian ever knew the truth. By then, water was thicker than blood, and they were a family, in all the ways that mattered. The Clark family.

Pauline was "Ma" from the beginning, in the present, and forever would be in the future. Standing almost as tall as Brian does, at a lofty five feet nine, she had wavy salt and pepper toned hair and smiling, Irish-green eyes that peeked out over silver wire-rimmed bifocals. And even though she was tall, she was just a little on the pleasantly plump side – due to her insatiable love for sweets and home baked goods like the delectable muffins she had brought Brian for breakfast. And although it was always rumored that Pauline was infertile, no one ever really knew why she and Jesse never had any more children. She never talked about it and contented to be an only child, Brian never asked for a sibling growing up. But since everything had happened with Emily, Brian was sure it was all part of God's infinite plan, for a time such as now, and he eagerly waited to see His plan unfold.

The cold hardwoods sent shivers through his bare soles as he followed Pauline into the kitchen, bumping up the thermostat in the hall on the way.

"Thanks, Ma" he said, pecking her ever so sweetly on her rouge-tinted cheek. "I'll go get dressed while the coffee's brewing.

"Heard from Emily?" she called to him as he disappeared down the hall and upstairs to the bedroom. He pretended he was out of earshot, but her question rang loud and clear in his head. He knew she was waiting for an answer. He knew she also already knew the answer, and wondered why she even asked. Pauline resented Emily for leaving, and was growing ever more tired of waiting for her to come home and be the wife she had promised to be to Brian in her wedding vows. Sure, she was sympathetic to Emily's loss, but felt her place was here – with her husband – who was also grieving the same loss. Still, she knew how much Brian loved her, and did her best be supportive and help him keep the faith.

"No, not a word" he yelled back, and then firmly shut the bedroom door, signaling to her that, like the door, the subject was quickly closed.

"She'll be back", he could hear Pauline's muffled response, even through the thick, wooden door.

Pauline was a "matter of fact" kind of woman. Nothing ever seemed to ruffle her feathers. Even when his father died, Pauline was brave and stoic, handling every detail of his death with dignity and grace. And even though his father made Brian promise to "make room" for Pauline when he died, she insisted on a place with detached quarters so she wouldn't be "a third wheel" living with him and Emily. She was a very independent soul, yet she seemed to thrive on taking care of them, as if she were performing one last unselfish act of love for her dearly departed husband.

Emily loved her too. For a while, they even shared the unspeakable bond of infertility, until Emily got pregnant. But even then, Pauline put aside her own shameful pain and celebrated a new life vicariously through Emily's expanding belly. They went baby shopping together, and Pauline accompanied her to doctor's appointments when Brian had to work. With Emily's own mother a hundred miles away, a surrogate mother bond was destined to happen between the two women. And as with the role of stepmother, Pauline fell eagerly and gracefully into the role of "grandmother to be". That's another reason she took it so hard when Emily left. She had invested her heart and soul into not only that of her surrogate daughter, but of her future grandchild, as well.

Then baby Jacob died. No heartbeat, the doctor said. Just like that. Something about a *chromosomal aberration-* a medical term that begged more questions than it answered. Brian punished himself for not going with her on that last appointment. He should have been there. Why didn't God urge him to go instead of putting it off on Pauline? Emily needed him to be there and he wasn't. Stupid job. It was his day off but he insisted on working overtime. For the baby. He was going to use the extra money to buy the nursery furniture Emily had drooled over in the furniture store. So Pauline offered to go. No big deal - just a routine check up. Just the week before, the baby was fine - weighing over four pounds, with a heartbeat as strong as a horse. What went wrong in just a week's time?

Emily spent countless hours pouring back over the minutes, hours, and days afterwards wondering what she had done wrong. Was it the extra onions she heaped on her salad? Or was it when she tripped going upstairs, even though she didn't fall? Did she worry too much? Eat too little? Stay on her feet too long? She had tried to do everything right, still it had to be SOMETHING. She needed there to be a reason besides *chromosomal aberration*. She needed something or *someone* to blame. And even though neither one really knew or understood what it meant, Emily insisted it was HER fault. In her family genes. Passed down on her side. She desperately wanted to take the blame and punish herself. And then she wanted to punish God for making her "defective".

Even at the funeral, she refused to bow in prayer, staring angrily instead at the ceiling as if to dare God to show up or try to comfort her. He was too late. She had prayed for a miracle but He chose to deafen his ears to her sobbing pleas. Like Job, she cursed the day she was born, as well as the day she conceived their son. Pauline even confided in her about a miscarriage she suffered when she was younger, but Emily refused to be consoled by anyone. She welcomed anger and bitterness inside like her best friends. And she shut her real family and friends out. Then she just up and left. Without a word of warning, she just left. No note, no explanation, no hope. A living suicide. She didn't even take a suitcase or change of clothes. One day, Brian came home from work and she was gone. He called everyone he could think of, including her best friend, Eva, and her sister, Carol. No one had seen or heard from her in almost a week. Then her mother finally called one night and said she knew where Emily was, but that she had sworn her to secrecy. Said she just "needed time".

"Leave her alone and she'll come back when she's ready", her mother coldly instructed us. *Leave her alone? Funny word, "leave". She's the one that left, yet we're the ones who are supposed to leave HER alone?* Brian thought. Didn't make sense. Then again, none of it did.

Dressed and desperately needing a strong cup of coffee, Brian finally returned to the kitchen. Pauline set a piping hot cup of coffee in front of him, along with a warm, cinnamon swirled top blueberry muffin - her specialty. The fresh aroma of coffee beans lingered in the air, as did the question she had asked earlier.

"She still not answering her phone?" Pauline asked.

"No, it still goes straight to her voicemail" Brian answered, as he slurped a large tongue full of hot coffee.

"I'm praying she comes home soon" Pauline sighed.

"Me, too, Ma; me too", Brian added, never looking up from his coffee and muffin.

"Well, I gotta get to the beauty shop, son. Oh, by the way, I ran into Roy Beacham at the post office the other day. Said he needs someone to help out on the Christmas tree farm this year during the holidays. His grandson won't be coming home from college this year to help like usual. Roy said he's going upstate to spend time with his girlfriend. I know he would appreciate a strong, abled-bodied fellow like you to help him out! Might not pay much, but it would get you out of the house a few hours a day. You should call him. Time you quit moping around this house and do something constructive!"

Subtlety was definitely not Pauline's strong suit. When she wanted to say something, she usually just did. And she was also usually right. In this case, she was more than right - she was insistent. Brian knew to argue with her would have been like arguing with a bobcat - claws speak louder than words! Besides that, his unemployment wasn't going to last forever. And the extra money would help him catch up on the medical bills left over from Emily's pregnancy.

"Sure, Ma, I'll give him a call. Can't hurt. I got nothing else to do. Might even be fun. Why, I'll have this place looking like Who Ville by Christmas! We'll have a Christmas tree in every room, and I might even put one in the dog pen for Babe and Pal!" he joked sarcastically.

Babe and Pal were Jesse's old hound dogs he used to take hunting with him. Course these days, they weren't much good for hunting - between the canine arthritis and cataracts, they wouldn't know the difference between a coon and a porcupine, much less have the energy to chase one! He glanced up to see if his sarcasm had offended her. She rolled her eyes back at his dry humor, as well as his feeble attempt at sarcasm.

"I'll tell Roy to expect your call, if I see him uptown. And tidy up this place if you get a chance - Pastor Gray is liable to show up tonight. It's his night to visit."

Pastor Anthony Gray led the Shelbyville Baptist Church, just two miles up the road. It was the largest church in Shelbyville. In fact, it was the ONLY church in Shelbyville. And with a population of only five hundred and fifty people, it stood to reason that Pastor Gray would make his rounds to your house at least twice a month. More so, if you were "on the prayer list". And Brian had been on that list ever since Emily left. In fact, sometimes he felt like he was the ONLY one on the list, as everyone in town had called or visited to pay their respects to "poor, jilted Brian".

"Sure, Ma, I'll straighten up a little. If I have time between cutting down Christmas trees and all." He gave her a smirky grin and a half-audible chuckle out of the side of his mouth. Pauline lovingly ruffled his sandy blond locks and gave him a light peck on the cheek.

"Just like your father - always cutting up. Glad to see

11

you're still smiling, though. I know you miss her, son."

The smirk left Brian's mouth and his expression turned to stone. Hard, cold stone. And Pauline knew to leave it alone. Sometimes all you can do is pray. And she did. She prayed for Brian and Emily, every day. She knew what it was like to miss someone. How she missed her Jesse! But her heartache was different. She had properly grieved her loss, and she knew that Jesse Clark was never coming back.

Brian, on the other hand still had strong faith that Emily could come back any day. How she hoped, for his sake, it was soon. *What was wrong with that girl, anyway?* Brian was the best catch in Shelbyville. Good looking, smart and a loving Christian husband. If Emily didn't come home soon, there were plenty of other unattached girls in Shelbyville ready to take her place! Already, they were wearing out the aisles at church each Sunday, wooing and consoling Brian, with future hopes of being the next *Mrs. Brian Clark.*

"I'll see you at supper, son. We'll just eat a sandwich since the Pastor's coming. Don't forget - call Roy!" Brian nodded and she ruffled his hair with her fingers once more, just as a reminder, and then headed for the front door.

"Thanks for the muffins, Ma!" he yelled back as she dashed out the front door.

Taking his coffee with him, he went back to the living room and sank down in his brown leather recliner, grabbing the TV remote from the table beside him. He turned on the TV to catch the morning news, flipping through the channels with repetitive fervor. It was part of his morning ritual now - a mindless means of procrastination. His eyes glazed over each program, as vivid thoughts of Emily wrestled for his attention. As hard as he had tried, he couldn't function without her. He didn't know how. They were so much a part of each other. When she left, it was as if she took him with her, leaving only his body behind. He may as well be dead like baby Jacob - at least that's how he felt inside. Without Emily, his life was cold and empty – and lonely. He was so lonesome without her!

Letting Go: Emily's Homecoming

He glanced over at their wedding picture on the old oak bookcase. She was so beautiful. Long, auburn curls cascading down her shoulders; big chestnut brown eyes, and a wide ear-to-ear smile that could light up the darkest sky. She was twenty-six. He was twenty-eight. They had been married for five years when she finally got pregnant with Jacob. As beautiful as she was as his wife, it couldn't begin to compare with the radiance she exuded as an expectant mother. As corny as it sounded, she really did beam with the proverbial "pregnancy glow" – the new life inside her lighting up their world with hope and expectancy!

Then baby Jacob died, and with him, Emily's glow. Snuffed out like a candle. At once, all the color drained from her face. Even her eyes seem to lose their color, changing from a sparkling beautiful brown to a mournful, hollow gray. She literally died inside out. As did Brian. They mourned together day and night. They shut out everyone and everything so they could privatize their mourning. Their home became a shroud of death, as containers of plants and flowers piled up outside the door, left there by well-meaning friends and neighbors. Sympathy cards poured in and pitying phone calls went unanswered, caught instead by the unobtrusive answering machine. Time stood eerily still as they wrapped themselves tightly in suffocating grief.

After the funeral, Brian suggested they take a trip somewhere -get away, maybe even move and start over. He reminded Emily of how in the Bible, after David's son died, he got up, went home, took a bath, got something to eat, and went to the temple and worshipped God. It was time to let go of Jacob, and go on with their lives. He knew it would be a hard step for her to take, but a necessary one in order to move forward. He also knew it would be easier to move on – together.

Instead, she cursed him for suggesting such a "heartless idea". She had an entitlement now. A right to mourn, for as long as she felt necessary. How dare he suggest she needed to "let go" and move on! She couldn't understand how he was so ready to forget their stillborn son, and go on with life, as if nothing had happened. She cursed him. She even slapped him. And she spit in the face of his faith. She mocked God and blamed him for causing Jacob to die. Then she threw up a massive wall around her grieving soul. No one was allowed in, and she made herself a prisoner so she wouldn't have to come out. Brian knew then he had lost her. And that's when she left.

After her mother called, he figured Emily must have been staying with her in Cherokee Hills - a little town about an hour away. It was her hometown. In fact, they had met there when he was working on a glass job at the Cherokee Hills Casino. Emily worked there as a waitress in the casino restaurant. His company had sent a work crew there for a week to replace a series of broken windows that had been damaged by recent snowstorms. Every day at lunch, he and the rest of the guys would pile in the Diamond Mine Restaurant for lunch and feast on everything from fried crawfish to petite filet mignon. Emily worked their table most every day, as they always left her a generous tip. Brian was instantly attracted to her bright, beaming smile and warm, friendly way. Even as the other guys ogled her and threw around hillbilly compliments, she brushed off their ill-fated attempts at picking her up with the grace of a royal princess.

Finally, on the last day they were there, Brian got up the nerve to ask her out for that weekend, to which she meekly accepted. On Friday, he made the hour-long trek to Cherokee Hills to pick her up and take her to the movies. From then on, they had a standing date every weekend for four months. Finally, he asked for her hand in marriage, to which she again agreed. They'd been together ever since. He brought her to Shelbyville to wed, and their new life together was as sweet as the maple gum trees that dotted the western hills of the Silver Ridge Mountains.

Emily and Brian attended the Shelbyville Baptist

Church (where they were also married), along with Pauline. After only two months, Emily gave her life to Christ, and was baptized. Brian even convinced her to join the choir after he heard her singing in the shower one morning. She had the melodic voice of a springtime songbird! She even sang solo a couple of times on Sunday during special services. She also started a Bible study for young men and women on Wednesday nights.

Meanwhile, Brian was stretching his own God-given talents as a part time youth pastor, ministering to the ten or twelve youth members who regularly attended there. Church was their second home, one with a revolving door. Brian even felt God might be leading him to further his spiritual education, and seek out a pastorate there, as Pastor Gray had been talking about retiring in a few years. But for now, it seemed God had a different plan, and Brian wasn't sure which direction his life was headed.

With Brian working overtime at the glass factory, Emily decided to stay home and take some online business courses to fill the long, empty hours while Brian was working. But after a while, the novelty of learning wore off and Emily was eager to start a family. But after two years, nothing was happening. Her gynecologist ran all sorts of tests and labeled her condition as "unexplained infertility". Brian as well, was put through all the usual "male tests", and passed with flying sperm, uh, colors. *"Relax"*, the doctor had said, as well as everyone else who had their own armchair medical degree. Of course, that was like telling a fly to be still-not likely to happen. Emily tried everything from homegrown chickweed to sleeping with a lock of hair under her pillow. Then again, her family was one-half Cherokee Indian. Ancient tribal Indian remedies had just about a good a chance of causing her to conceive as modern medicine when the diagnosis was "unexplained".

Unexplained also described how Emily finally got pregnant three years later. No one knows, except of course,

God - and He's probably still laughing about the hair under her pillow! When the ultrasound finally revealed it was a boy, Brian was prouder than a full-plumed peacock. A son. It was also what Emily had hoped for. Boys were "easier" to raise, she had said. Brian suggested they name him "Jacob", after the favored son of Isaac in the Bible. Emily liked the name, too. No more discussion was needed. Jacob Jesse Clark would be their first child!

It was a fairly easy pregnancy for Emily. She suffered only mild morning sickness, and on her lanky five foot six inch frame, you could hardly tell she was pregnant. Still, baby Jacob grew and grew, right on schedule. Ultrasound after ultrasound confirmed a healthy baby and an uneventful pregnancy. And with the exception of a half-trip up the stairs, Emily took exceptional care of herself while she was with child. In fact, she did all the right things, exerting maternal caution at every corner. Like refusing to take an antacid when she overindulged on pasta at Marietta's Italian Restaurant. Said she didn't want the baby to have acid reflux before it was even born! No, she wasn't obsessive, just cautious - as any expectant mother would be. She did everything right by the book. At least she thought she did. That's what made it all so wrong. That's why it hurt so much. That's why it didn't make sense. And that's why she left.

After Jacob died, nothing made sense anymore. She not only questioned God, but she questioned everything else, too. Even her marriage to Brian. She decided since Jacob died, the rest of her life would die too. At least that's how Pastor Gray explained it to him. Emily didn't know to just grieve the loss of her child. She couldn't separate him from the rest of her life because she had made him her life. Getting pregnant and having a child was the central most important thing to Emily. Baby Jacob was an extension of her life – the umbilical cord of life connecting her to the world around her. Made sense that when he died, so did the rest of her life. Except where did that leave Brian? Now he had not only lost a son, but a wife, too.

Would Emily ever be able to let go of Jacob and come back into the loving arms of the man who loved her more than life itself? Would she ever be able to separate herself from her grief, and be a whole person again?

Brian slowly picked up the phone on the table beside his recliner. He let out a big sigh, and then dialed the number. After three rings, he was just about to hang up when a gruff voice answered.

"Yea, this is Roy Beacham"

"Roy, this is Brian Clark. Hear you might need some help down on the tree farm this year?"

"Sure do Brian, you interested? Can't pay you much but its steady work through the holidays."

"Yea, I'm interested. Don't care much about the pay - still getting some unemployment. Just need something to fill in the gaps, you know?"

"Well, be here at eight in the morning, then. Gotta truck coming in for a load -should be a good day's work. Won't be any gaps in this business – at least not 'til after Christmas!"

"You got it, Roy. Sounds good. See you in the morning."

Brian hung up the phone and reached down for the lever on the recliner. He slowly reclined back and stared at the dusty gray wooden ceiling beams above him. Looked like it would be his last late night of keeping vigil for Emily. His life was moving on. Moving on without her. But only physically, as she would be forever and foremost in his thoughts no matter where he went, or what he did. And in his prayers. Certainly, she would always be in his prayers. He wondered though, had Emily moved on too? Maybe moved on without HIM?

CHAPTER 3

"*B*rian! Brian!" a familiar voice called out from outside the window by his chair. Realizing he must have dozed back off to sleep, he jumped up like a hooked catfish on dry land. He stepped over to the window to see who was beckoning him so bright and early. It was Gracie Hawkins, the local mail carrier.

Gracie was in her early sixties with wispy, silver-black hair that stretched all the way down to her waist. She was also Cherokee Indian, and suffered from the bizarre delusion that she was Cher, the famous female rocker. She even had *I Got You, Babe* tattooed down her right shoulder. To say she was a little eccentric would be putting it mildly. However, she had been delivering mail in Shelbyville for the past twenty-two years, without fail, and everyone loved her, including the local dogs, as she always gave them Carob Canine Candy treats when she delivered the mail each day. And even though no one ever figured out who "Babe" was, she could have had her pick of any mutt or sooner in all of Shelbyville!

He hurried outside to collect the mail. Bills, no doubt, as that was about all that came since his unfortunate exit from the employment world. That, and his meager unemployment check – which would be running out before Christmas!

"Hey there, Brian, baby, what's happening?" Gracie asked; whipping her willowy silver-streaked hair to the side in typical "Cher style", while handing him a small pile of mail.

"Nothing much, here Gracie - same ole' same ole', you know."

"How's your Ma?" she asked, sorting through her mailbag to make sure there wasn't anything more.

"She's good, thanks for asking", Brian replied, while simultaneously flipping through the assortment of bills, letters and sales papers she had handed him. He cringed as he waited for the question that seemed to always follow from everyone – *heard anything from Emily?*

"Well, you people take care - see you tomorrow, Brian, baby! Peace out!" she said, holding up her fingers in a "V" format and waving bye. Brian returned the gesture, as she cranked up the volume to "Gypsies, Tramps, and Thieves ", which blasted loudly from the mail truck as she sped on down the road. *That's funny – she didn't ask about Emily! Guess she was in a big hurry today. Thank God for small miracles. Now if He'd just perform a bigger one – and bring Emily home!*

He turned to go back inside when he noticed a familiar handwriting on one of the letters sticking out from the pile he held in his hands. No return address. He looked closer. Could it be.... Emily's handwriting? His heart begin to beat a little faster as he tore into the letter like a kid opening a birthday present. He sat down on the second step of the front porch and began to read:

Dear Brian, I'm sorry I haven't been in touch. I know you are worried and upset, and wondering where I am. I hope you can try to understand why I had to leave, and how very hard this is for me. You'll have to forgive me - I guess I just can't bounce back as easy as you can. I felt like you were pushing me to get over Jacob's death, and I don't think that's fair. Everyone grieves in their own way and time. I also am not ready to just "go on" with life, as you say. I need to figure out exactly HOW and WHERE to go, without him. You just don't understand, Brian, because you're a man. You didn't give birth to a dead baby after almost nine months of feeling life inside you! You can't possibly know how I feel or what I need right now. And it's strange because he was YOUR son, too. I don't understand how you can just let him go so easily, and so soon. Anyway, I just wanted to let you know I'm okay. I'm staying with Mom until I can sort things out. Please don't come here. I need time and I need to be alone and figure this out myself. I'll be in touch. Love, Emily.

Brian crumpled the letter and balled it up tightly in his hand. Anger welled up inside, but love fought to the surface. Her words hurt but the thought of her going through such a traumatic loss alone, hurt more. *Maybe if I go anyway, she'll be glad to see me. Maybe she'll come back home with me if I go and convince her to come back home. Maybe I can help her through this better if we grieve together.* He was her husband - she needed him. And he needed her. This distance thing was crazy! He had tried SO hard to be patient with Emily after the baby died – not push her too hard – just enough to help her on with her life. But he never meant to push her completely away – or completely out of his life! Feeling helpless defeated and even more discouraged, he hung his head and through tear-blurred eyes, sent up a desperate prayer: *Lord, help me help Emily. And help me, too; God help us both get through this!*

Through his tears, his eyes caught the return address on another envelope: *Heaven On Earth Memorials.* It was addressed to *Mr. and Mrs. Brian Clark.* He slowly opened the envelope and took out the enclosed letter. It was a bill for the memorial stone Emily had ordered for Jacob after he died. *The Jacob Clark memorial stone is ready to be shipped, pending approval of an attached proof.* He shifted to the proof on the second page. It was an image of a bluish gray granite heart, etched with Jacob's name and birth/death date. Below that was an oval cut out for a photo, covered with a piece of acrylic to encase the picture. A scripture verse was etched at the bottom:

"Let the little children come unto me..." (Matthew 9:14 KJV) The instructions were to check the appropriate box after viewing the proof. *APPROVE* if the information on the proof was correct, or *CHANGES NEEDED* if something needed to be changed.

Emily needed to see the proof. She had insisted on ordering the memorial stone after Jacob died to put on his grave. Maybe this was the perfect excuse to go see Emily. Surely, she would want to see the proof and make sure everything about the stone was right. Then again, maybe not. She was already devastated over losing Jacob. This would just upset her even more. Maybe it would be better if he just ordered it for her and put it on Jacob's grave, then take her to see it when she came home. And she WOULD come home. He just had to believe that one day God would bring her home.

He looked back over the instructions. *Changes must be requested within five days or stone will be shipped AS IS. Please remit check or money order for total amount due with proof.* He glanced down to the bottom to find the amount due. $549.95. *Whoa, that was a costly piece of rock!* There was no way Emily had that kind of money right now. And he certainly didn't have it, not with being laid off and only drawing unemployment. He'd have to ask Pauline for a loan. And she'd lend it to him, he was sure. After all, it was for Jacob. And Pauline was as upset over losing him as they were. After all, it would have been her first grandchild. And a boy at that. Pauline had always wanted a son, she had told Emily many times. It was this sacred sisterhood bond that she and Emily had formed, that made him so sure it was all in God's hands. And even though he didn't understand the senselessness of all that had happened, he knew Pauline would be a big part of the healing process.

Returning inside, he put the rest of the mail on the antique roll back desk in the hall, to be tended to later. He carried the memorial stone bill and laid it on the kitchen counter. He'd talk to Pauline about it when she came home for dinner. He took Emily's crumpled letter, which he had shoved in his pocket, carefully smoothed out the wrinkled pages, and read over it once again. *I need to be alone....*

That's where she was wrong, Brian decided. She needed to be home with her husband. Letting him share and help her through her pain. She needed to be with people and friends who could support her and love her back to a meaningful life again. A life without baby Jacob. And most of all, Brian needed her. Not just for him. But so he could do what he promised God he'd do when he spoke his wedding vows. *In sickness and in health, for better or for worse…* How could he stand by her if she wasn't there? How could he honor his vows to a wife that shut her husband completely out? He neatly folded the letter and tucked it back in his shirt pocket. He knew he'd read it again a dozen more times before nightfall…

It was going on ten-thirty and Brian still hadn't tidied up the house as Pauline had requested. He looked around the living room. Newspapers and junk mail littered the floor and coffee table. His dirty work boots were lying haphazardly by the fireplace, dried leaves and grass still clinging to the soles. A soiled and smelly sock peeked out from under the tongue of each shoe. A half finished glass of OJ sat on the side table beside his recliner, a dead fly floating on top. The dust on the mantle over the fireplace coated the once glossy, polished oak wood with a thick grayish-white film. *What in the world was Pauline carrying on about? The place didn't look THAT bad,* he asserted, with typical male reasoning. Still, he knew it would never pass the "Ma Clark inspection!" Better tidy up a bit!

Normally, Emily would have the cabin looking like a five-star hotel. She always was an immaculate housekeeper. Of course, she did slack off somewhat after her sixth month, but even then, she was fastidious about picking up Brian's dirty socks and leftover drinking glasses, scolding him the whole time about being so sloppy and untidy. And even though, like any man, he hated to hear her nag at him, he'd give anything if she were there to fuss at him now. Anything.

He sank back down into his recliner, took out Emily's letter, and read it once more. Her words cried with unbearable pain and heartache. Brian's own tears began to fall as he read. He was finally beginning to understand Emily's pain – from her perspective instead of his own. He thought about another mother who bore the unfathomable pain of not only losing her son, but watching Him die a tortuous death, nailed to a splintery old wooden cross. Mary, the Blessed Mother of Jesus lost her Son, too. But her son came back to life after three days – the greatest miracle of all times! Mary got her miracle – Emily didn't! Unless… God had another miracle in mind for Emily and Brian – like maybe another son – or daughter! But how could they create another child together if Emily wasn't there?

Brian knew he had to go and bring Emily home – if only he could get her to let go of her past – maybe, there would be a miracle in her future!

CHAPTER 4

"*I* got a letter from Emily today", Brian told Pauline at dinner later that night.

"Well, it's about time - when's that girl coming home where she belongs?" Pauline's words were sharp, her questions pointy. She couldn't have been any more protective over Brian if she had given birth to him himself!

"She didn't say - just that she needed time. Said she didn't understand how I could get over Jacob's death so easy. She's still hurting, Ma - hurting badly."

"And she doesn't think YOU are? What's wrong with that girl? We're ALL hurting over losing Jacob - doesn't she realize that? She's being pretty selfish if you ask me!"

Pauline got up and started clearing the table. She was visibly annoyed and upset with Emily's unwillingness to come home and share her pain with her husband - and with her. The careless way she slung dishes into the dishwasher was a dead giveaway. Being a woman that faced her fears and her enemies head on, Pauline didn't have a lot of patience for someone who insisted on wallowing in her pity pot!

"She'll come back when she's ready, Ma. I know God will send her home. She just needs time to heal. I won't lose faith in her just because she's lost faith in me, or God or anyone else. Besides, there's something else I got in the mail today - something I hope you can help me out with". He walked out to the hall and got the bill from the memorial company, and handed it to Pauline.

"This came today, too. It's the bill for Jacob's memorial stone. I can't afford to pay for it right now, Ma, and I'm sure Emily can't either. Can you loan me the money 'til I get back on my feet again?"

24

Pauline slid her glasses from the top of her head, and over her eyes. She took the bill out of the envelope and stared down at the *Total Due* column: *$549.95.* Laying the bill on the table, and without saying a word, she retrieved her checkbook from her purse, scribbled out a check to *Heaven on Earth Memorials* for the full amount, and handed the check to Brian, then continued cleaning up the dinner dishes.

Brian gave her a quick, sweet peck on the cheek. "Thanks, Ma, I'll pay you back, soon as I can." He folded the check and stuck it in his shirt pocket. He'd attach it to the memorial form, and give it to Gracie in the morning when she came by to deliver the mail. Maybe by the time the memorial stone arrived, Emily would be home. Maybe it would help bring a little more closure to the gaping wounds of her heart, which were still oozing with pain and sadness.

Babe and Pal's incessant barking coming from outside alerted Brian that Pastor Gray had arrived. He met him at the door while Pauline fixed a pot of coffee.

"Hi, Pastor, please come in. Ma will be right out - she's just getting some coffee for us. Please, have a seat."

Pastor Gray was a distinguished looking man with a head full of silvery gray hair and a thinning grayish moustache. His six foot two frame was lanky and slim, with the exception of a slightly protruding belly - the result of too many helpings of Mrs. Watson's homemade banana pudding at the monthly Wednesday night family suppers. He carried a black leather Bible, its golden leafed pages slightly faded and turned up at the corners. He sat down on the edge of the sofa, holding his Bible loosely between his gaping knees.

"So how are you, Brian? I've been praying mighty hard for you, son - and for Emily. Any word yet?"

"Thanks, Pastor - as a matter of fact, I got a letter from her today. She's staying with her mom up in Cherokee Hills." He looked down at the floor, and then looked back up at Pastor Gray, tears filling his eyes.

"Said she needs time…, said she doesn't understand

why I'm not hurt and bitter like she is...., " He stopped, rubbed his forehead and wiped the tears from his eyes. He got up and faced the window, his back toward Pastor Gray.

"She still blames God, Pastor Gray - and me and even herself. She' so full of hurt I don't know how to help her."

"Come over here and sit down, Brian. Let's see what we can find in God's Word to guide us in this situation."

Brian pulled his handkerchief from his back pocket, blew his nose, and took a seat in his recliner. Pastor Gray flipped methodically through the gold-trimmed pages of his Bible. The worn, crinkled pages made a crisp, snapping sound as he flipped them a couple more times, then finally stopped at the book of Ecclesiastes. Adjusting his glasses just a bit on his nose, he read slowly, yet with a boldness and confidence, as if he were King Solomon himself speaking:

"To every thing there is a season, and a time to every purpose under the heaven: A time to be born, and a time to die; a time to plant, and a time to pluck up that which is planted; A time to kill, and a time to heal; a time to break down, and a time to build up; A time to weep, and a time to laugh; a time to mourn, and a time to dance." (Ecclesiastes 3:1-4 KJV) He slowly closed his Bible, slid his glasses back up on his head, and looked over at Brian.

"Don't you see, Brian, it's time to let Emily go? Not just physically, but emotionally and spiritually. You have to let her go so God can heal her. It's not meant for her to be here right now otherwise she wouldn't have left. You see, Emily has to let go of Jacob, and she can't come back to you until she's done that. But you've got to let go of her first because you're getting in the way of what God needs to do to heal her. It's His job, Brian, to heal Emily - not yours. And it's all in HIS time, not yours. Let her go, son, and trust that God will bring her back when the time is right."

Brian put his head in his hands and sobbed. Months of hurt, confusion, and anger poured sweat from his pores like a torrential rainstorm. He needed to let go of more than just

Emily - a lot more. Even though Emily thought he had so easily let go of baby Jacob, he knew that he was holding onto his dead son just as tightly; as well as the dreams he'd had for their future. Dreams of playing baseball, going fishing and taking him hiking up the Silver Ridge mountains. He not only mourned losing a son – he mourned the loss of being a father.

Pauline came out with the coffee and set it on the TV tray Brian had set up by his recliner. She reached over and held Brian's head against her side. "It's alright, son, let it out. You got a right to cry." She looked over at Pastor Gray.

"You see what that girl has done to my boy - that was HIS baby too - don't you think he's grieving his son's death, too? She's only thinking about herself – that selfish girl!" Pauline was as protective as a mother bear over her cubs when it came to Brian - Emily or no Emily. Even still, she was in just as much pain as Brian. Emily was the daughter Pauline could never have, and it hurt deeply that she didn't lean on her for support after the way they had bonded so easily when she got pregnant.

"I know, Pauline, you're all hurting over this. And I'm telling you the same thing I just told Brian - let Emily go. She's no good to any of you right now. And neither you nor Brian can fix Emily. The Lord needs time with her - you've both got to let go and let God heal Emily - and you and Brian, as well."

Brian pulled his head away from Pauline's embrace, blew his nose, wiped his tear stained face, then got up, and went out on the porch. The chilly late November air nipped at his cheeks and nose – another biting reminder of Emily's icy departure.

"Want a cup of coffee, Pastor?" Pauline asked.

"Thank you, Pauline, I'd appreciate that." Pauline poured the Pastor a cup of black coffee and a cup for herself, and then sat down on the sofa beside him.

"I'm worried about him, Pastor. Emily has turned his world upside down. He's lost a son, a wife and now a job. How much more does she think he can take?"

"Brian's a strong man, Pauline. He has a lot of Jesse Clark in him – don't forget that! Just be patient with him and try to help him stay encouraged. And get him back to church. Everyone misses him – especially the youth. It would do him good to get his focus back on God's work, instead of moping around waiting for Emily to come home."

"I've tried, Pastor. He says he just don't feel like being around those young people right now – reminds him too much of the son he lost. He won't admit it, but he's taking this harder than anyone realizes. He's lonely. Real lonely. And I know Brian; he's not going to wait on that girl forever! I just hope he can hold until she gets herself together. Otherwise, she may come back and find herself an EX-wife!"

"Well, unfortunately, some marriages aren't strong enough to survive such a tragedy as this - especially a tender, young marriage such as theirs. It's true; the longer Emily stays away, the less chance there is of her coming home. This is one case where distance doesn't necessarily make the heart grow fonder!" Pastor Gray explained.

"But I don't think you have to worry about Brian; his constant love and faithfulness to Emily shines as bright as the snow-glistened Silver Ridge Mountains! I don't believe for one minute he would ever be unfaithful to Emily, much less betray his wedding vows to God – he's a better man than that, Pauline!"

"Well, I hope you're right, Pastor Gray, I really hope you're right!"

CHAPTER 5

"*J*ust lop about four inches off the bottom, trim the scraggly lower branches, and then toss it into the bagger. Sally will collect the money from them in the Christmas shop while you're loading up the tree for them", Roy instructed Brian the next morning at Beacham's Christmas Tree Farm.

Sally, a short, pudgy woman of about sixty-five, was Roy's wife, and ran the Sugar and Spice Christmas shop right beside the tree lot. Together, she and Roy had been selling Christmas trees in Shelbyville for nearly forty years. Nothing was as pretty the day after Thanksgiving, as the road coming 'round Silver Ridge Mountain Road into Shelbyville that led to Beacham's Christmas Tree Farm!

For three whole miles, bright red bows and colorful twinkling lights lit up the mountainside, while Christmas music rang all over Shelbyville from the seventy- five foot tower of the Shelbyville Baptist Church! It was like being in Who Ville, minus the grumpy old Grinch, of course! And customers came from as far away as Cherokee Hills to buy a "Beacham's Best" Christmas tree – the freshest smelling Frasier firs in the Silver Ridge Mountains!

With all the nervous energy he had stored up since Emily left, Brian chopped, trimmed and loaded Christmas trees like one of Santa's elves on Christmas Eve! By eleven o'clock, he had sold over fifteen trees and dulled two chain saw blades. Not to mention, drank a half gallon of fresh homemade apple cider! By lunchtime, he felt a little like a cross between Johnny Appleseed and an Irish lumber jack! The work was steady and exhausting, but it was just what he needed to take his mind off Emily – at least for a while.

While Roy took over, Brian took a much needed and

well-deserved lunch break. As he chewed on the BLT Pauline had made him for lunch, his thoughts raced quickly back to Emily. Everything inside him wanted to pack a bag, jump in his truck, and high tail it to Cherokee Hills – just like he had done all those weekends he went to see Emily when they were dating. How he wished he could go back in time, start all over again with her, and rewrite history. And even though he wouldn't change a lot, he would definitely rewrite the past few months. If only he could.

If only Emily would just let it all go, as Pastor Gray said! If only she would let go of the pain. Let go of the blame. And let go of Jacob. He was in God's arms now – his Heavenly Father. And Brian knew one day they WOULD see their son again, and hold him - not as a dead stillborn baby, but as a happy, healthy, carefree little boy full of life and love. But Emily wasn't willing to wait until then. She wanted Jacob to be in her arms NOW. She resented the fact that God was holding him instead of her. And even though Brian understood her anger and bitterness, he understood that God's thoughts are *"not our thoughts; neither are His ways, our ways"*. (Isaiah 55:8 KJV) He learned a long time ago that where understanding left off, faith took over. But Emily had yet to get to that point. All she knew was that Jacob was gone and in her mind, God was to blame. *"Let her go."* Pastor Gray's words came bouncing back like a giant rubber ball thumping around his mind's wall. *Easier said than done,* he grimaced back at the intruding thought.

"Brian, you 'bout done with lunch; the truck is here for a load of trees!" Roy beckoned from around the corner.

"Yea, I'm done. Be right there" he called back, thankful for Roy's interruption of his depressing thoughts.

For the next two hours, Brian chopped and loaded Christmas trees into a long eighteen-wheeler semi whose destination was none other than Cherokee Hills! How ironic – here he was loading trees to be delivered to the same town he met Emily! It seemed no matter which way he looked, there was some kind of reminder – even on Beacham's Christmas tree farm! How was he ever supposed to *"let her go"* with all these constant reminders?

Finally, the truck was loaded and Brian was exhausted from a full day's work. He could already feel the warm, massaging spray of a hot shower before dinner, and a restful night's sleep ahead. And even though his back, neck, and shoulders were already aching from the toilsome labor he had already endured the first day, it was a welcome change from the emotional pain he had endured since Emily left. This kind of pain he could just take a couple of aspirin and be better the next day. But the emotional pain of losing a son, a wife, and a job required much deeper therapy - and a whole lot of prayer!

*P*auline already had dinner fixed for Brian when he returned home later that evening. Sage-seasoned meatloaf, buttery mashed potatoes, and red-peppered green beans for the main course, and Pauline's homemade pecan-crusted apple pie for dessert. Mountain apples had been plentiful in Shelbyville that year, apparent from all the apple-spiced cider and apple-laced desserts Brian had indulged in over the past few weeks! If *an apple a day keeps the doctor away*, he was sure he wouldn't need a doctor anytime soon! It was just as well. With no health insurance, and all the bills that his previous health insurance didn't pay from Emily's pregnancy, there was nothing left over for doctor visits anytime soon!

But he knew God would provide. He always had, and He always would. As mixed up as he was about Emily, he stood fast in his faith. He knew God was the ONLY one he could rely on, and his faith was something he was NOT about to let go of! In God's time, Brian knew, *this, too, shall pass.*

"How'd it go today?" Pauline asked as she set a huge helping of beefy meatloaf and steaming mashed potatoes in front of Brian at dinner.

"Tiring. But it felt good to work again. Thanks, Ma, for

telling me to call Roy. It feels good to be needed again, too."

Pauline knew he was referring to Emily. Brian was the kind of man that "needed to be needed" and it was obvious that Emily didn't need him to help her get through losing their son. But Brian needed her to need him, and she couldn't even give him that. The more Pauline thought about it, the madder at Emily she got. In fact, she had half a mind just to go to Cherokee Hills, find Emily, and shake some sense into that girl! But she knew Brian would be madder than a bear in a beehive if she did, so she just tried to stay out of it best she could. She, too, remembered Pastor Gray's sage advice to "*let Emily go*".

"Glad it's working out so well for you, son. I know you are a big help to Roy and Sally, too. God put you both in each other's paths for a reason. In His time, He'll work everything out. It's all in His timing. Things will work out – you'll see", she said, remembering Pastor Gray's advice to keep Brian lifted up and encouraged.

"I know, Ma; I know" he garbled, in between forkfuls of mashed potatoes.

After dinner, Brian reared back in his leather recliner and before long, was sound asleep. Pauline finished the dishes and fixed Brian a Tupperware container of leftovers to take to work the next day. Tiptoeing lightly by, she laid fifty dollars on the side table beside Brian's chair, kissed him on the forehead, and quietly eased out the front door, as his contented snoring wafted throughout the empty house.

*B*rian had only been asleep about an hour when he was jolted awake by his cell phone ringing. Groggily, he reached over, picked it up and looked to see who was calling. It was Roy.

"Yeah, Roy, what's up?"

"Hey Brian – sorry to disturb you this late but something's come up and I need a huge favor."

"Sure Roy, what is it?"

"Sally's brother just had a massive heart attack, and I'm afraid he didn't make it. We need to leave tonight for Rocky Mountain, to go be with the family and make the funeral arrangements. I wonder if you could help Willie out at the tree farm for a few days for me? My niece, Karla, is going to come over and help out, too. She knows how to run that Christmas shop almost as good as Sally. I'd sure appreciate it if you could stay on and help them out 'til I get back! "

"Oh, I'm sorry to hear that, Roy. Please give Sally my condolences. And of course, I'll be glad to stay on and help 'til ya'll get back! Take as much time as you need – I'm sure Karla, Willie and I will get along just fine!"

"Thanks, Brian. It sure is great how God just sent you my way – guess He knew I'd be a' needing you right about now. Oh, and don't worry about the evenings - I've already talked to my brother Ed. He and his wife, Sara, and their son Chad will come in relieve you, Willie and Karla. We'll be back soon as we can."

"No problem, Roy. Take care and ya'll drive careful!"

Brian got up, stoked the fire a couple more times, and then headed on up to bed. He stopped by the medicine cabinet in the bathroom and downed a couple of ibuprofen, in preparation for the muscle aches he was already sure he would awaken with the next morning.

As he lied down in the downy softness of his king-sized bed, it occurred to him that for the first time in weeks, he was actually sleeping in his bed instead of the couch. Amazing how one day of hard, manual labor, can make a body yearn for the comfort of a bed – even an empty one! Too tired to wrestle with his usual thoughts of Emily, he quickly succumbed to a peaceful night's rest

CHAPTER 6

Karla Beacham was a petite, dishwater-blond-haired woman of about thirty, with a mischievous smile that twinkled as happy as the red and green lights that dotted the Christmas trees at the entrance to Beacham's Christmas tree farm! She was Roy's sister Margaret's only child. And a spoiled one at that. When Margaret passed away a few years earlier, she left Karla quite a substantial inheritance. Both her parents were retired from the military, and true to traditional military family style, Karla was a spoiled military brat. She had been taking care of Margaret since her father passed away, and now that her mother was gone, she was a very RICH spoiled brat.

Nevertheless, ever since she was a child, she loved hanging out with her "Uncle Roy-Roy, and Aunt Sal" at the Christmas tree farm. She worked there just about every year as a teenager until she went to college and dawdled away four years trying to "find herself". But all she found was more ways to spend all the inheritance money her father had left her. And now that Margaret was gone too, she had even MORE money to throw away! Still, she would do anything for Roy and Sally, and she was glad she was able to help.

"Hi, I'm Karla – you must be Brian!" she cheerily welcomed Brian when he arrived for work the next morning.

"Hi Karla – yep, I'm Brian, A.K.A. *"The Lumberjack"!* Brian replied, with a bashful laugh. Karla chuckled at his comic reply and stuck out her hand.

"Nice to meet you, Mr. Lumberjack!" She gripped Brian's hand tightly and he winced at the great power this tiny woman possessed in her small, delicate hands!

"Same here" he smiled back, her hand still clasped snugly in his. And although it was just a handshake, it felt strange; strange to be holding another woman's hand – even if it was just to shake it. He quickly pulled his hand away from hers and slipped them both securely in the front pockets of his overalls.

"I'm so glad you're here to help Uncle Roy and Aunt Sally out like this! You know, this is their busiest time of the year and they'd be in a mess if they had to close the tree farm right now! You're really a God-send!" She pointed to the sky as if she were personally thanking God for sending him.

"Well, I'm glad to do it. Worked out good for me, too. I've been out of work for a couple of months now, so I can really use the money myself!" Brian replied.

"Oh really, well, it looks like God's timing was just right, then, huh? You know what the Bible says' *"To every thing there is a season, and a time for every purpose under the heavens:"* (Ecclesiastes 3:1 KJV) She lifted her hands to the sky once again, as to accentuate the verse of scripture she had so beautifully just quoted.

"Well, someone certainly has been studying their Bible. Care to take on a little friendly Bible challenge sometime?" he asked.

"Sure – but I must warn you – I lead a Bible study group at my church each week, and Bible scripture is kinda required reading, if you know what I mean!" She laughed another cutesy laugh that brought out two well-defined dimples at the bottom of each rosy pink cheek.

"Oh, yea? What church do you attend?" Brian asked.

"Shelbyville Baptist. I just joined about a month ago. They needed someone to take over the Wednesday night Bible study group, so I volunteered. I heard the woman that was teaching it left town or something."

Brian's head dropped and his face went blank with a "doe in the headlights" look. Emily was the one who had taught that class, but gave it up after Jacob died. In fact, Brian had given up his part-time youth pastor position, too. It was just too painful for both of them to see all those happy, smiling faces of the young boys and girls, knowing their own child never got a chance to live. Pastor Gray had been urging Brian to come back to church, but he wasn't ready yet. And not without Emily. He'd hoped he could convince her to come back with him when she came home. And she WOULD come home – it was just a matter of time. Just like Karla said – when the season was right.

"Brian, is something wrong?" Karla asked, noticing his change in demeanor. "Did I say something wrong?"

"No, not at all" he lied, trying to avoid opening up the subject of Emily. "I'd better get to work, though - we'll have customers coming in soon, and I need to change the blade on the chain saw. I better head on out to the lot." Without looking back up, he shuffled off, leaving Karla just a bit puzzled at his abrupt departure.

Brian breathed a sigh of relief as he quickly headed out to the lot. It was too early in the morning to get into all his personal drama with a woman he barely knew! Besides, she'd find out soon enough from the some of the busybodies at church about him and Emily. There were always two or three that just LOVED to gossip about other church members, despite Pastor Gray's many sermons on "busy jaws, loose tongues, and sharp ears"!

*T*he morning went by quickly and by lunchtime, Brian was starving. He handed the chainsaw to Willie, and asked him to take over so he could grab a quick lunch. Willie, an older man of about sixty-five, had also once run his own Christmas tree farm, but lost it during a severe drought that hit the state one year. With no crop insurance or money to buy more trees, Roy gave him a job, and he'd been there ever since. It was just another example of how God took one man's loss and turned it into a double blessing - a job for Willie and an extra hand for Roy. Brian could only hope God would do the same for him and Emily.

Pauline had packed Brian leftover meatloaf and

mashed potatoes for lunch, and his mouth was watering just thinking about the aroma of hearty beef with tangy tomato sauce, and creamy butter-drenched mashed potatoes. He'd left his lunchbox in the refrigerator in the Sweet and Spicy Christmas shop, where Karla waited on tree customers and sold other Christmas goodies like apple cider, spiced muffins and decorative wreaths made from the cut off Christmas tree branches.

"Lunch time already?" Karla asked from behind the cash register when Brian walked in to retrieve his lunch.

"Yea, 'bout time, too – I'm hungry as a mountain bear!" he replied with half a smile.

"Mind if I join 'ya?" Karla asked.

"No, not at all, but I'm afraid I didn't bring enough for two!" Brian replied, hoping to discourage her self-imposed invitation. He still didn't feel like engaging in any personal conversation – especially with the woman who took Emily's place at the Bible study group.

"Oh, that's okay – I've got a ham biscuit I didn't eat this morning. It'll fill a hole!" she joked. She quickly grabbed a Coke from the fridge and parked herself at the wooden picnic table Roy had put in the back of the store for the customers. Brian shoved his takeout tray of meatloaf in the microwave and pushed the REHEAT button, while Karla feasted on her biscuit.

"So, I'm ready to take you up on the Bible challenge anytime!" Karla said. Brian pretended not to hear her remark over the loud whirr of the microwave. She raised her voice even louder and repeated herself, shouting over the microwave.

"HEY - I SAID, I'M READY FOR THAT BIBLE CHALLENGE NOW!" The bell dinged on the microwave and Brian removed his food and sat down at the table across from her.

"No offense, Karla, but I've only got about ten minutes to eat so I can relieve Willie. I'll have to take a rain check on that Bible verse thing, okay?" he replied through the foggy steam of his mashed potatoes.

"Sure - sure thing, Brian." Karla replied, as she slurped the last swig of her Coke and tossed the biscuit wrapper in the nearby trashcan. She cast Brian a confused look, then got up, and went back to the front of the store. Although she had just met him, her instincts were razor sharp and she knew he was kindly telling her leave him alone. *Fine. If that's how he wants to be, I can take a hint! What's his story, anyway,* she wondered.

Brian finished his lunch and started for the door, but a tinge of guilt stopped him in his tracks. He felt bad about his curt remark to Karla, and knew he needed to apologize. Backing up a few steps, he inched back inside, turned around, and stared blankly at Karla, who was now standing at the register totaling some receipts from the morning's sales.

"Look, Karla, I owe you an apology. I'm sorry I was so short with you earlier when you said something about the Bible challenge. It's just that I've got a lot on my mind and, well, I need to focus on doing a good job for Roy. I hope you understand – I really didn't mean to come off sounding so rude. Will you forgive me?"

Karla studied his face for a moment, and could almost see the weighty burden he was carrying hidden behind his furrowed brow and weary eyes. ***"Be kind to one another, tenderhearted, forgiving one another, as God in Christ forgave you."*** (Ephesians 4:32 KJV) The familiar scripture verse from Ephesians quickly came to her mind. She had just taught about it at Bible study a couple of weeks ago. She didn't need to know the reason; all she needed to do was forgive.

"Of course, I forgive you; no need to apologize – or explain. And you're right – I shouldn't distract you from your work. I'm sorry, as well!"

"Oh, its okay – like I said, I've been going through some stuff and I guess I'm just not very talkative these days!" He gave her a clumsy smile, then threw his hand up and waved. "I really should be getting back so Willie can eat his lunch. I'll talk to you later, okay?"

"Sure, Brian; anytime. I'll be right here!" She smiled sweetly and held both hands out, palms up to gesture her whereabouts for the rest of the day. Brian returned the smile and once more headed out the door, just as the phone ringing diverted Karla's attention away.

"Merry Christmas! Beacham's Tree Farm; How may I help you?" she cheerfully answered.

"Hi, honey, it's Uncle Roy. How's it going?"

"Oh, hey, Uncle Roy. Everything's fine here; how's Sally and the family?"

"They're holding up pretty well, considering. Sally's mom is taking it kind of hard. That was her baby boy, you know. Gonna take her some time to accept it. Sally might stay up here an extra week or so with her, but I'll be coming home by the weekend. Can you stay on and help me and Brian out 'til Sally comes back?"

"Sure, Uncle Roy. No problem. You tell Aunt Sally to take as long as she needs. I'll be more than happy to stay on."

"Oh, that's great, Karla. She'll be so relieved. You know she hated to leave me in a bind. You don't know what a blessing you and Brian BOTH have been in all this!"

"Glad to be able to help out, Uncle Roy. After all, since Kevin and I broke up, I needed something to fill in all this extra time on my hands!"

Kevin, Karla's boyfriend of all of three months came and left as mysteriously as snow in July, and that's when Karla decided to come home and roost at the old home place for a while. Margaret had left her the big farmhouse in the valley about three miles away, but it had just been sitting there since Margaret died. Roy had hoped Karla would find a good man and settle down for once in her life. Maybe if she could stay in Shelbyville long enough, she'd have a better chance of that happening!

"Oh, by the way, I don't mean to be nosey or anything, but what's up with this Brian dude? He seems to be dealing with something pretty heavy."

One thing Roy would have to say about Karla – she didn't beat around the bush when she wanted to know something! Got it from her Mama. Margaret was the nosey one in the family and in this case, the apple didn't fall far from the tree! He suspected her question was more than just "friendly interest". That girl was always on a manhunt, and it looked like Brian Clark might be her next prey! Better to divert her trail sooner than later!

"Well, to be honest, Karla, Brian and his wife are going through a pretty tough time. They just lost a baby boy a few months ago. A stillborn. They're both taking it real hard; Brian could really use your support – and prayers!"

"Oh." Karla's voice immediately changed to a more serious tone. She certainly didn't want Uncle Roy to think she had eyes for a married man!

"That's really sad. Of course, I'll keep them both in my prayers. And you and Aunt Sally, too! Don't you worry about things here; Brian, Willie, and I have it all under control! You be careful coming home, okay?"

"Thanks, sweetie; I will. See you in a few days!"

Karla slowly returned the cordless phone to its cradle, and tapped her bony fingers across the wooden counter. *So THAT'S his story!* Her eyebrows arched like the Eiffel Tower, and a devilish smile slowly crawled across her face like a ghoulish Halloween spider. *Poor Brian. I'll bet it was HIS wife that used to teach the Bible study group! Someone said she had lost a baby and was real depressed! Tsk! Tsk! She shouldn't leave a grieving husband all alone after something like that. No, he needs someone to console him, cook for him, and comfort him. After all, doesn't the Bible say to "bear on another's burdens"? It WOULD be the "Christian" thing to do, now wouldn't it?* She laughed a wicked laugh under her breath, and licked her lips seductively. And even though it was closer to Christmas, it looked like Brian Clark was going to be an unsuspecting fly caught in somebody's deadly Halloween web!

CHAPTER 7

*P*auline heaped two pieces of country-fried pork chops on Brian's plate at dinner that night. After a long, hard day of chopping trees, she knew he'd be as ravenous as a grizzly bear. He definitely got his healthy appetite from his father! Oh how she used to love to cook for Jesse Clark- and watch him eat! He'd savor each bite, all the while declaring how she was "the best cookin' mountain wife" in the Silver Ridge Mountains! God, how she missed that man!

"How's it going down at the tree farm so far, son?"

"Busy, Ma - real busy. Willie and I didn't even have time to take a break this afternoon – customers just kept coming! With school out now for the holidays, all the parents are bringing their kids in to pick out the Christmas tree. Looks like Roy's gonna have a record year!"

"Well, I know he'll be glad to hear that! By the way, I understand his niece Karla is helping out at the farm while they're away?"

"Yea, she's there. Met her this morning. Seems nice, but likes to talk a bit too much for me! Oh, by the way, did you know she's the one that took Emily's place teaching the Wednesday Bible study group at church?"

"No, I didn't. But I had heard someone new had taken over. Did you tell her you were Emily's husband?"

"Nah – I didn't feel like getting into all that with a total stranger, Ma. Besides, what difference does it make? Who knows if Emily will be coming back to Shelbyville anytime soon, much less back to church to teach a Bible study group? Pastor Gray had to have someone take over – I'm glad Karla was able to step in. She seems to be knowledgeable about the Bible, anyway. She quoted a few Bible verses, so I guess she's qualified to lead a Bible study group –don't you think?"

"Quoting scripture doesn't mean a person is "qualified" to teach God's Word, son. There's a lot of so-called "men and women of God" that are really devils in sheep's clothing! Besides, I'd keep my eye on that girl if I were you. Lila Stokes told me Margaret had her hands full with that girl since her husband died. Said she took her Daddy's money and ran off with some man to California for a few years, then came home when she found out Margaret was on her deathbed. Came home to make sure she got her inheritance – I'm sure! Now that she has that, she'll probably get up with another man and run off again!

"Oh, Ma, you know Lila Stokes – she's such a talker! She's had something to say about everyone in Shelbyville at one time or another! Maybe she ought to spend more of her time talking about the Lord!"

Lila Stokes was Shelbyville's town gossip, and Brian had about as much use for her as a rusty saw. She was the kind of "Christian" that went to church just so she could get enough gossip to "curl" all the local ladies hair at the beauty shop each week. My, how those busybody hens liked to sit around Flora's Beauty Shop and peck at people on Saturday mornings!

"Besides, Ma, that was years ago. The girl hasn't been around in years, so how does Lila Stokes know so much about her? Maybe she's settled down now and turned her life around! People DO change, you know!"

"Okay, son, I'm just passing along a little friendly warning. The girl sounds like a man-chaser to me. And if she gets wind that you're a lonely, grieving husband whose wife just up and deserted him, she might just set her sights on you! Just be careful, Son – remember Delilah in the Bible? She shaved Sampson's head when he wasn't looking! Don't let the same thing happen to you!"

"Okay, Ma, I'll make sure to keep my cap on when I'm around Karla Beacham!" he said sarcastically. He ripped the last piece of meat off his pork chop with his teeth, washed it all down with a few gulps of tea, and finished with a swipe of his napkin across his mouth.

"Besides, Ma, I'm STILL a married man who's very much in love with my wife, and who WILL be back home one day. One day SOON, I hope. I ain't interested in any other woman – and especially not Karla Beacham!" He pushed away from the table and patted his bulging stomach. His shoulder muscles ached and his head was begging to sink down in the downy feather pillow on his bed. If tomorrow were going to be anything like today, he would need all the rest he could get.

"I think I'll go on up to bed now, Ma. I'm dead tired. Thanks for supper – it was delicious! You're still the best cookin' mountain Mama in the Silver Ridge mountains! Don't forget to leave the porch light burning when you leave." He gave Pauline a quick peck on the cheek and trudged wearily up the stairs to bed.

His sweet compliment warmed her heart – just like his father used to do. Like father – like son...

"I'll remember. Sleep tight, Son – love ya", Pauline called out to the shadow of footsteps he quickly left behind.

"Love you, too, Ma – 'nite!" he tiredly called back.

Pauline cleaned up the dishes, fixed Brian a plate of leftovers for lunch the next day, and then left to go back home, locking the cabin door behind her, and leaving the porch light burning, just as Brian had insisted. Burning for Emily.

A glowing orange ball peeked from behind a faintly pink-tinted sky and over the lofty Eastern hills of Shelbyville early the next morning, its long golden fingers stretching in and arousing a sleeping Brian from his near comatose state. He rolled over to escape the unwelcome morning intruder, but glaring streams of light mercilessly pried open his eyes and sent blood pulsing through his veins. The bedside alarm clock followed suit with its untimely and incessant beeping.

"Oh, alright, I'm up, I'm up" Brian grumbled to the electronic noise box. He flicked the alarm off, pulled himself up to a sitting position on the side of the bed, and rubbed his face several times with his hands, trying to stimulate the blood flow back to his brain. He noticed a slight chill in the air and quickly grabbed his robe from the foot of the bed. *Ma must have forgotten to bump the heat up,* he guessed. Probably on purpose, though. She was always reminding him to keep the heat turned down so the electric bill wouldn't be so high. Funny, he never needed the heat up when Emily was there!

He lay back on the bed and closed his eyes. He could just feel Emily laying there beside him, her soft, willowy figure curled up next to his. Sometimes they used to lie in bed for hours on the weekend, talking and snuggling, or making love and basking in the sweet afterglow. Her presence warmed not just his bed, but the whole house, as well. She was the fragrant candle that made the whole house glow with life and beauty. But now that she was gone, there was nothing left but a cold bed, an empty house, and Brian's broken heart.

He opened his eyes and glanced over at the clock. Less than an hour to get to work. Somehow, he was thankful for the cold air that once again rudely slapped him in the face. There was no reason to stay home anyway. Not without Emily there. He quickly showered and changed, grabbed the leftover pork chops Pauline had left for him in the fridge, and shot out the door into the brisk, cold morning.

Cranking the '87 Chevy truck his Dad had left him, he revved the engine a few times to get the motor going. He flipped the heat on and rubbed his hands together briskly between his legs. By now, the sun was perched full and high above the towering blue mountains, radiating Shelbyville with a trillion megawatts of solar energy. *Maybe today will be the day Emily comes home*, Brian wistfully thought. *Yea, it could be today!* The spirited thought carried him cheerily all the way to Beacham's Christmas tree farm.

"Morning, Brian!" Karla sweetly called out to him

when he came into the shop to put his lunch in the fridge.

"Morning, Karla. How are you?" He smiled politely, but not too encouraging, remembering what Pauline had told him the night before. Just in case.

"Fine, thank you. And you?"

"I'm good – just not quite used to getting up so early again!" He laughed just a little, just to let her know he was in a better mood than the day before.

"Yea, I know what you mean – it would be nice to sleep in on these cold, lonely mornings, wouldn't it?" she replied quite forwardly.

"Oh, by the way, I brought lunch for us today! I hope you like bean soup – it's my specialty! And I made a loaf of homemade bread to go along with it! I remembered how hungry you said you were after cutting down all those trees, and a hot bowl of my bean soup will give you some much-needed energy! Oh, and for an afternoon snack, I brought us some homemade chocolate chip cookies!"

"Good Lord, you must have been up cooking all night!" Brian said. "But I hate you went to all that trouble because I've already got something for lunch!" He held up the Tupperware container with the leftover pork chops for Karla to see.

"Oh, well, that's okay. You can still have a bowl of soup, can't you? Doesn't look like you've got much there to eat, and a big, strong muscular lumberjack like yourself needs LOTS of good carbs for fuel!" she suggestively replied, her eyes lustfully roaming up and down his brawny physique.

"Yea, I guess I could eat a bowl of soup along with my pork chops. Thanks, Karla. That was very thoughtful of you, but don't feel like you have to do that every day! Ma usually cooks for me and she always cooks enough for me to have leftovers the next day! I'm sure I won't go hungry!"

"Oh, it's no bother. I LOVE to cook. Besides, you can take the soup home and freeze it for later. You know, just in case you need a hot meal one night and *"your Ma's"* not there." The words dripped sarcastically from her tongue.

"By the way, Uncle Roy told me about what happened to you and your wife. I'm really sorry, Brian. I'm sure it's hard not having a wife around to take care of you anymore." Once again, she teasingly batted her eyes and poked out her lips in a pouty stare. Brian suddenly felt very uneasy in this woman's presence.

"I've got to get to work now, Karla," Brian replied, cautiously heeding Pauline's earlier warning.

"Sure thing, hon' – I'll heat the soup up for you when you're ready for lunch!" she called out, as Brian quickly left, slamming the door behind him. He'd have to deal with her later. Right now, customers were piling in and he knew Roy was depending on him to sell as many trees as possible. Besides, he had enough to worry about without Karla Beacham adding to the mix!

With a steady stream of customers coming in, Brian and Willie worked tirelessly throughout the morning. Four busy hours rendered seventy-five trees chopped, trimmed and hoisted on tops of cars, in beds of trucks and straddled between luggage racks atop SUVs. Every house in Shelbyville would boast at LEAST one of Roy Beacham's Christmas famous trees, with plenty more traveling as far north as Maine and even Canada! Still, it WAS just a seasonal business, and Brian knew Roy was counting on selling every mature tree that was on the farm. The hot, summer months to come would not be forgiving to the ones left to survive another season.

Noon finally rolled around, and although he dreaded another encounter with Karla, Brian was too famished to skip lunch. He marched into the Christmas shop and headed straight to the back to retrieve his pork chops from the fridge. Thankfully, Karla was busy waiting on a little old lady trying to decide between a jar of homemade apple butter or blueberry jam as a Christmas gift for her daughter. Maybe he could quickly get a cold pork chop down and a glass of iced tea before she got through, hoping the little old lady would take up just a few more minutes of her time.

Forgoing a hot meal, he choked down the cold, dry pork chop and washed it down with a few gulps of sweet tea from a Mason jar Pauline had packed along with his lunch. He was just about to take the last bite when Karla's customer finally made up her mind. She chose the homemade apple butter, and Karla quickly rang up her purchase and bagged it in a Christmas themed brown paper bag. Within minutes, she was rid of the dawdling customer and scurried to the back to meet up with Brian.

"Hey, ready for some of that soup now"? she asked Brian excitedly as she reached for the handle on the refrigerator to retrieve the soup.

"Actually, Karla, I just finished off a pork chop and it was kind of big. I think I've had a plenty for now. But thanks anyway. Why don't you go ahead and have some, though."

"Oh darn – I was hoping you'd share a bowl with me!" She curled up her lip and twisted her mouth in a disappointed look.

"Sorry Karla, maybe some other time. I gotta get back to work. There are still a lot of customers on the lot!" He gulped down the last of his tea and shoved the empty containers back in his nylon lunch bag. He started for the door, then stopped and turned back around. Once again, God nudged him about his rudeness to Karla.

"Hey, Karla... maybe I will take a couple of those chocolate chip cookies for a snack later, though!" Karla's eyes lit up as she danced over and grabbed a Ziploc bag of cookies from atop the microwave.

"Here you go, sweetie" she brashly replied, swinging the bag of cookies back and forth in front of Brian's face.

"Hope you like 'em – the chocolate chips are EXTRA big!" She stared boldly into Brian's eyes; her seductive message bluntly delivered. Brian hesitantly took the bag of cookies. He felt a warm glow of embarrassment spread across his cheeks. It had been so long since a woman had shown any interest in him, he felt like a shy schoolboy again. He felt the blood rush through his lower extremities. He caught a gentle whiff of Karla's sweet-smelling perfume. Or maybe it was just the chocolate chips from the cookies. He couldn't tell. But something was definitely teasing his senses.

Caught off guard and unable to speak, he quickly turned away and bolted out the door. The thoughts that followed him were just as confusing: *I shouldn't be having these feelings; I'm a married man....*

CHAPTER 8

*B*rian flipped through the stack of mail he had pulled from the mailbox later that afternoon when he got home from work. Nothing but bills. And not another word from Emily. He unlocked the door and threw the mail on the hall table as he headed to the kitchen. His eye caught a note lying on the counter.

Brian, I had to run over to meet Nellie at the church to work on the costumes for the Christmas pageant. You'll have to fend for yourself tonight, Son. Love, Ma.

Pauline had really spoiled Brian since Emily left. She cooked dinner nearly every night, as well as tended to his laundry and tidied up the house whenever she could. But the Shelbyville Baptist Church Christmas pageant was just a few weeks away, and Pauline and church-member Nellie Bigford had been in charge of mending and re-sewing the used costumes each year for twenty-two years. It just wouldn't do for one of the Wise Men to show up at the Christ Child's birth with torn sleeves in his robe! No, Pauline and Nellie would see to it that every costume was in respectable condition and nicely pressed before the pageant.

Brian opened the fridge to see what leftover offerings might be lurking there. A quart of two-week old curdled milk stared back at him, along with a half-opened pack of chicken bologna. *Time to do a little grocery shopping,* he sighed. He shut the refrigerator door and decided to go pick up a burger down at Rusty's Grill - Shelbyville's most popular hamburger joint. In fact, it was Shelbyville's ONLY hamburger joint. Being so far up in the boonies it wasn't likely you'd find any golden arches peeking out over these mountaintops!

Smart move ole' Rusty Chisholm made ten years ago – putting a hamburger joint at the foot of the mountains! The golden arches wouldn't stand a chance against Rusty's even if they DID open up in Shelbyville! Brian's mouth watered just thinking about a beefy grilled cheeseburger, topped with Rusty's famous mountain chili and sautéed onions!

Grabbing his jacket from the hall closet, he flipped on the porch light, and started for the door. Just about that time, a knock was heard coming from the other side. *Must be Pastor Gray,* he thought, knowing how preachers like to make impromptu visits and at the most inopportune times! He opened the door expecting to see the Pastor, but was face to face with Karla Beacham instead.

"Karla... what are you doing here?"

"Hey, Brian, you going somewhere?" she asked, noticing the truck keys in his hand.

"Well, yea, as a matter of fact, I was headed out to get something to eat. Is there something I can do for you?" He looked down and noticed she was holding a large woven picnic basket.

"Oh, don't do that!" she sweetly begged. "I brought you some of that bean soup you didn't get to eat at lunch today, and some home made fried chicken. I figured that with Ms. Pauline helping out at the church tonight, you wouldn't have a good hot meal to come home to! *How did she know Pauline was at church tonight?,* he wondered.

"Well, that's very kind of you, Karla, but really, you shouldn't have gone to all that trouble. I was just going to go down to Rusty's and get a burger." He caught a whiff of the fried chicken – his favorite dish! Once again, taste buds did somersaults in his mouth as the aroma of freshly fried chicken permeated the doorway. Even as good as Rusty's was, a burger couldn't hold a candle to crispy, deep-fried chicken and hot, homemade bean soup!

"Oh, it was no trouble, Brian. All I have to do is heat up the beans; the chicken is still hot and fresh from the deep fat fryer!" She fluttered her long, dark eyelashes at him and shifted from foot to foot, flirting for an invitation inside. What could he say? He relented and invited her in.

"Well...okay – sounds good, I guess - c'mon in, Karla. You'll have to excuse the house, though, it's kind of in a mess." She quickly brushed by him looking from room to room for the kitchen.

"The kitchen is all the way to the back", he pointed, following quickly behind. She made her way to the stove and started searching through cabinets looking for pots and pans.

"Uh, all the pans and stuff are right there" he said, pointing again to a cabinet by the stove.

"Oh, I'll manage to find them. You just sit down at the table and I'll have this stuff heated up for you in a jiffy. You got something to drink?"

"Yea, I think there's some iced tea in the fridge. Would you care for a glass, Karla?" he asked, retrieving the tea pitcher from the refrigerator.

"Sure. Thanks. The soup should be ready in a few minutes. I know you must be starving, as hard as you worked at the lot today! Shame you didn't have a nice hot meal to come home to after a long hard day's work" she replied in a pitying and highly sarcastic tone.

"I really appreciate this Karla, but really, you didn't have to bring me supper. I ain't used to nobody cooking for me, 'cept Ma. And I can pretty well fend for myself if she's not here!"

"I know, but I enjoy it. You know, since Mother passed, and my boyfriend left, I don't have anyone to cook for, so it makes me feel like I'm... you know... needed." She turned around just in time for Brian to see a lone tear fall from the corner of her eye. This woman knew all the moves, and she was playing Brian like a barracuda!

"Oh, I'm sorry. I remember how tough it was when Daddy died. It must be even harder losing both parents" Brian replied, trying to sound sympathetic.

"Yes, I miss them both terribly" she sniffed. She placed a bowl of piping hot bean soup in front of Brian and sat down across the table from him. "Well, dig in, while it's still hot!"

"Aren't you going to join me?" Brian asked.

"No, I've already eat. But I'd love to sit and visit with you while you eat, if you don't mind." Again, what could he say? It wouldn't be right to take her food, and then ask her to leave!

"Uh, no. That's fine. You're welcome to stay while I eat; but don't let me hold you up if there's something else you need to be doing", he replied, hoping she wouldn't stay long.

"Nope, nothing. Unfortunately, there's no one waiting at home for me, either." Once again, she batted her eyelashes and let out a big, pitiful sigh. Brian couldn't help but cast a disapproving eye back.

"Oh, I'm sorry. I didn't mean to imply anything. I know you couldn't help your wife leaving you. Still, I imagine it gets pretty lonely around here, too, huh?" Brian put down the spoonful of soup that was about to cross his lips. He stared down at the bowl and prayed that God would help him say the right thing to such a wrong comment. He looked back up at Karla and stared her straight in the eye.

"Look, Karla, I'd really rather not discuss my personal life with you, if you don't mind. My wife and I have a lot to deal with and it's just not something I want to talk about, okay?" He picked up his spoon and continued eating. The space between them became tense and awkward. *Why couldn't I have left for Rusty's just five minutes earlier*, he thought as he hurriedly slurped down his soup.

"Hey, I'm sorry Brian. I didn't mean to pry. I can't imagine what you're going through – what you're BOTH going through. But I'm here if you DO decide you want to talk. You know, sometimes it helps to talk to someone who's unbiased. Helps you see things from a different perspective, you know? You take my situation, for example. My boyfriend, uh, EX-boyfriend, Kevin…"

"Excuse me, Karla," Brian interrupted", finishing his last spoonful of soup, "but it's getting late and I'm really bushed. Would you mind very much leaving now? I think I'm gonna call it a night. I'll save the chicken for lunch tomorrow. Thanks again for the supper."

He got up and set the soup bowl in the sink, along with the empty lunch containers he had put in there earlier, and ran some hot water over them. Karla, seeing an opportunity to stick around a little longer, rushed to the sink and pressed her body close to his.

"Sure, Brian, I understand. But here, at least let me clean up these dishes for you before I leave. It won't take me but just a minute and then I'll be on my way." She started filling the sink with dish soap and water, and began sponging them clean. Too tired to argue, Brian walked away, letting her have her way.

"Suit yourself. Just put the leftovers in the fridge, and if you don't mind, how about lock the door when you leave? And please, leave the porch light on, will ya? Thanks."

"No problem, hon'. You go on up to bed and get some rest. Gotta make sure our lumberjack gets plenty of rest!" she laughed. Brian stood there for a minute, wondering if he should let her stay, then remembered what she said earlier about wanting to feel needed. What harm would it do to let her wash a few dishes? Satisfied he was doing the Christian thing, he went on upstairs to bed.

Within a few short minutes, Karla had cleaned up the dishes and put the leftover chicken in the fridge. As she closed the refrigerator door, she caught a glimpse of a picture of Brian and Emily, on the door. She removed the picture from the magnet that was holding it and held it up for a better look. *So, that's what she looks like, huh? Kind of plain looking. Wonder what he sees in HER? Well, it shouldn't take long to get his mind off her... and on ME! Not long at all...*

She placed the picture back haphazardly on the refrigerator and nosed around the kitchen for a bit, looking for anything else to use in her scheme to lure Brian into her malicious trap. Not finding anything, she wandered through the hall and eyed the bills Brian left laying on the desk. She picked them up and shuffled through them, like a detective looking for clues. *Looks like he's behind in a few bills. Maybe he could use a loan until he got paid from Uncle Roy. Yea, maybe I'll just be a "Good Samaritan" and help poor Brian out a bit.* With all the money her mother had left her, Karla had more than enough to buy whatever she wanted, or WHOMEVER she wanted, as the case may be. And who said money COULDN'T buy happiness? Or a husband, for that matter?

She carefully put everything back in place and got ready to leave. As she passed by the stairs in the hall, she stopped and looked up. Knowing Brian was upstairs, all alone in his bed was too much temptation. Quickly and quietly, she tiptoed to the top of the stairs and paused. She knew Pauline and Nellie would be working on the costumes until late. An opportunity like this might not come again so easily! She scurried down the hall, cautiously peeking in each room until she finally found Brian in the room at the end of the hall. She closed the door behind her and softly walked to the side of the bed. Brian was fast asleep and snoring lightly. How she longed to slip into bed beside him and nestle in the security of his strong arms and manly chest!

Her inner thighs grew warm and tingly as she slowly starting unbuttoning her blouse. She closed her eyes and could just taste the sweetness of Brian's lips exploring every inch of her body. She dropped her blouse to the floor, unzipped her jeans, and quickly shed them to the floor, as well. Quietly and deliberately, she slipped in bed alongside Brian. Within seconds of feeling her warm body against his, he leaned over and began kissing her, pressing his lips deep against hers, his tongue finally forcing them apart to explore her mouth. After a few minutes, she felt his tongue leave her mouth and continue its journey slowly down her neck.

"I was hoping you'd come up" he whispered softly in her ear. "I've wanted you so badly!" She arched her back and moaned in contented pleasure as he continued to caress and explore each part of her quivering body.

"Oh, Brian, I've wanted you, too, baby! Please make love to me all night!" she begged, lost in the fiery passion that was quickly heating up between them.

Suddenly, Karla heard Brian let out a restless snore. She opened her eyes, her sultry daydream quickly fading away. Looking down, she realized she was still standing at the top of the stairs. Quick as a white-tailed doe dashing through the mountain woods, she hurried back down the steps, flipped on the porch light and ran out the front door. For now, her daydream would have to wait. But if her conniving scheme worked, it would not be for long! Not long at all!

CHAPTER 9

*P*auline slathered a piece of toast with warm apple butter, and set it atop the plate of bacon and scrambled eggs.

"Breakfast is ready, Brian!" she yelled to the top of the stairs. Within seconds she heard her son's heavy footsteps moving around upstairs, and a few minutes later, bounding down the steps.

"Where'd the fried chicken and soup come from? I know YOU didn't cook it last night!" she chuckled.

"Karla Beacham brought it over." He didn't bother with an explanation, although he knew one was expected.

"Oh? Well, wasn't that mighty neighborly of her?" Pauline pointed out sarcastically.

"Don't start, Ma – it was just a friendly gesture. She had brought the soup to work for me yesterday but you had already packed the pork chops for me. And somehow, she knew you were over at church with Ms. Nellie, and thought I might not feel like cooking, so she brought me supper. And that's ALL it was to it!" Pauline looked at Brian and shook her head in disbelief.

"Brian Clark – if me and your father ain't brought you up with no more sense than that, God help you! Living in the mountains like you do, I'd think you'd know a snow job when you see one! And it looks like that girl has already got you snowed six feet UNDER!"

"Ma – don't start!" he warned, shooting her "the look". She knew to let it alone – and least for then; however, this was one matter she'd definitely be bringing up again! Brian hurriedly downed his breakfast, hoping to avoid another lecture from Pauline so early in the morning.

"I gotta get to work now. Thanks for breakfast, Ma." He kissed her quickly on the cheek, grabbed his leftover chicken from the fridge, and headed out.

As he drove to the tree farm, he skimmed the radio channels to catch up on the morning news. The auto-scan dialer stopped on a Christian radio show he and Emily used to listen to on their way to church on Sunday mornings. It was like "church before church" service. He stopped the scanner so it would tune into the station. The speaker was quoting from 1 Corinthians.

"And unto the married I command, yet not I, but the Lord, Let not the wife depart from her husband. But and if she depart, let her remain unmarried or be reconciled to her husband: and let not the husband put away his wife." (1 Corinthians 7:10-11 KJV)

Brian switched off the radio. Even the Bible plainly states that a wife shouldn't leave her husband. He thought about what Pastor Gray had told him – that Emily had to let go of losing baby Jacob, and that Brian had to let go of Emily. But so far, the only one Emily had let go of was Brian. And how was he supposed to let go of the woman he vowed to love, cherish, honor, and protect the rest of their lives?

He pulled into the lot at Beacham's and parked. Karla was already there – her flashy red Corvette parked over by the Christmas shop. What a spoiled brat! Working for her Uncle Roy the past few days was probably the most work that girl had ever done! More and more, Brian wished she'd never come to help out!

"Hi there, Mr. Lumberjack," Karla greeted Brian as he went in the shop to put away his lunch.

"Morning, Karla." He caught a strong whiff of perfume as he walked by her, the spicy, alluring scent taking his senses by surprise. He glanced over at her and noticed she had worn her long, auburn hair down; soft, bouncy curls cascading freely around her face and shoulders. As his eyes traveled down, he noticed how her well-toned figure accentuated the stonewashed denim blues she was wearing, in ALL the right places. One thing was for sure; he couldn't deny she was a very attractive young woman! He felt a dull longing in his loins. After all, he was still a man. And Emily's absence had left him not only hurt and confused, but wrestling with a loss of sexual intimacy, as well. How much longer did she expect him to go without the affections of a loving wife?

Karla felt his eyes roving over her and inched closer to him - the desperate hunter moving in on its unsuspecting prey.

"I hope you enjoyed dinner last night, Brian. I really enjoyed cooking for you. As a matter of fact, I'd like to do it again tonight! I've got all the fixings for a scrumptious homemade pizza! And I'll bring my pizza stone so it will cook up just like an authentic Italian pizza! Say around seven-ish?" she asked, brazenly inviting herself over again.

"Uh, that won't be necessary, Karla. Ma will be home tonight, and besides, Pastor Gray is supposed to come by and visit. Maybe some other time, okay?" Her offer was tempting – pizza was another of Brian's favorite foods! But he knew Pauline would have a holy cow if he allowed Karla Beacham to come over again – especially knowing how she and Lila Stokes felt about her!

"Okay, no problem. Maybe another time, then? In fact, why don't you come over to my place Friday night and I'll cook it for you then?" Her invitation was sincere, but dripping with ulterior motives. Brian knew he shouldn't cave in, but what harm would it do? It had been a while since he'd had a good pizza – why not take her up on it? His answer slipped out before he could rationalize it any further.

"Well, okay…sure. Sounds good. Still want to say around seven?"

"Seven is great! Oh, and by the way, do you like wine or beer with your pizza? I have both, as well as some harder stuff, if you know what I mean!" she replied with a sharp wink.

Actually, Brian had stopped drinking after he met Emily and started attending church with her. In his wilder, more carefree days, it was nothing for him to kill a twelve pack of beer on a Saturday night, but since he settled down into married life, and started going to church, he'd lost his desire for that kind of lifestyle. And about the only time he'd tasted wine was when they had Communion at church – and even then, it was diluted with water – a request made by the mothers of the church so the younger members could partake without developing an alcohol addiction! But what harm could a beer or two do with a couple slices of pizza?

"Beer will be fine – whatever you've got is okay with me. I'm not a big drinker," Brian confessed.

"Me, either, really" Karla lied. "But it does go better with pizza, don't' you think?" She fluttered her long lashes at him and winked again. She was about as subtle as a mountain landslide!

"Yea, it does," he answered. "Better get to work now. See ya at lunch."

"Sure thing, Brian. Have a good morning! Don't work too hard, now!" she sweetly cooed as he walked out the door.

The morning shift passed quickly and business was brisk. It was almost noon and Brian was famished. Looking forward to the cold, leftover fried chicken he had brought with him, he hurried back to the Christmas shop. As he rounded the corner of the shop, he noticed Pauline's SUV parked outside. *Wonder what Ma's doing here? Maybe she's heard from Emily*, he thought excitedly. He swung open the shop door and saw Karla and Pauline sitting at the picnic table in back. *Uh-oh – this can't be good. Hope she's not giving Karla a hard time about coming over last night.*

"Hey, Ma – what are you doing here? Is everything okay?"

"Oh, hi, son; no, everything's fine. Just thought I'd come by and meet Roy's lovely niece, here! We've just been sitting here chatting and getting to know each other a bit. And I was just telling Karla about all the eligible BACHELORS in Shelbyville. I'm sure she'll find the right man if she just keeps looking, right Karla?" Karla looked up at Brian and rolled her eyes. It was obvious Pauline was an unexpected AND unwelcome visitor!

"Uh, right, Ms. Clark. If you'll excuse me, though, I need to go make up some more wreaths. I'll let you and Brian visit over lunch." Karla quickly retreated to the front leaving Brian and Pauline alone.

"Okay, Ma – what's going on between you and Karla?" Brian asked suspiciously.

"Nothing going on, son; just wanted to make sure Karla knew that you are a happily married man, and that there is plenty of available eligible bachelors right here in Shelbyville for her to pick from."

"Ma – please tell me you didn't give Karla a hard time!" Pauline pulled Brian closer to the back of the shop.

"Look, son, I told you to watch out for that girl. I'm convinced after spending just ten minutes with her that she can NOT be trusted! And if you're too blind to see it with your own eyes, maybe I need to point it out to you! She has her sights set on YOU, and she's not the kind to politely go away if asked. I'm just letting her know where the boundaries are between you and her."

Even though it upset Brian that Pauline was meddling in his personal affairs, he couldn't be mad at her for looking out for him. She made a promise to his father she'd always take care of Brian and that's exactly what she intended to do. Whether she knew it or not, Karla had her hands full if she intended to tangle with Pauline Clark!

"Look, Ma. I'm a big, grown man, and I can see very well what Karla Beacham is up to. But you've got to trust me to be faithful to Emily. I'm not about to do anything to jeopardize my marriage – not with Karla – not with ANYONE!"

"Then why are you going to her house for pizza Friday night?" Pauline asked.

"Oh, she told you about that, huh? Well, to be honest

with you, Ma, I happen to like pizza – and I feel kind of sorry for Karla. She doesn't have anyone since her Moma died, you know. Did it ever occur to you that she just might be LONELY? What kind of Christian would I be if I didn't extend a friendly heart to her? Maybe she just needs someone to talk to!"

"Are you REALLY that naïve, Brian? Even an old half-blind woman like Lila Stokes can see through all the smoke and mirrors that girl puts up! What's wrong with YOUR eyes?"

"I told you, Ma, I have NO intention of letting anything happen between me and Karla! Now would you please just back off and leave that girl alone? Maybe we should be trying to win her over to the Lord's side instead of throwing her under the bus, you know!" Pauline shook her head in disdain and threw her hands up in defeat.

"Okay, son. You win. But don't say I didn't warn you. Don't come crying to me when Emily comes back and finds you in the arms of another woman!"

"Oh, Ma, stop it! Wanna stay and have lunch with me? I've got enough of the chicken Karla cooked last night for both of us?"

"No thanks, Son. That's forbidden meat you're eating. I just hope you got sense enough to stop before you get to the forbidden fruit!" Pauline picked up her bag and walked to the front. Karla threw up her hand and waved as she walked by, but Pauline ignored her gesture and just kept on walking. She walked to the back and sat down while Brian ate his lunch.

"You're Mom's very protective of you. I think it's sweet!"

"Yea, well, that's just Ma. I hope she didn't offend you or anything."

"No, like I said; I think its sweet of her to worry so much about her son. She's just concerned because your wife has been gone for so long. She said she wished you'd get out more so I told her I was cooking dinner for you Friday night. I think she was glad that you were going to go out for a change."

Brian knew it was all lies, but didn't want to let on that he knew Pauline felt very differently. Something spoke to Brian in his spirit. He felt the need to get closer to Karla – not in a romantic way, but more in a spiritual way. It was like God was telling him to let go of the distrust he had for her, and share his testimony with her. Who knows if anyone had ever witnessed to her before? Sure, she said she taught the Wednesday night Bible study, but was she REALLY a Christian? Certainly her actions did not show it. Or maybe Brian and Pauline were misreading those too? Maybe Karla was put in his path for a reason. He couldn't be disobedient to God and walk the other way.

"Karla, are you still teaching Bible study on Wednesday nights at church?" Brian asked. His question caught her off guard.

"Uh, yea, why?"

"I thought I might start coming back. I don't know if you knew this or not, but my wife, Emily, used to teach that class." He waited for her response to a question he already knew the answer to.

"You know, it seems like I DO remember hearing that somewhere" she replied, acting surprised. "But I didn't know her – she had already left before I joined the church. But it would be great to have you join us! We start around eight. Why don't you come tonight?"

"You know, I think I will. It might do me good to get back into it again. I really enjoyed it when Emily taught it – there's so much in God's word to learn, don't you agree?"

"Yes, I do. And it will be so much more fun to learn it *together*. I'll look forward to seeing you there tonight, then!" The bell on the front door alerted her to a customer.

"I better get back up front. See you tonight, Brian!" She smiled a big smile and sashayed off to the front.

It would be interesting to see how well Karla taught the

Bible study, Brian decided. It would also give him a chance to see if her Christianity was from the heart, or if she was just a *"female Pharisee"*. He checked his watch. He still had a few minutes before he had to relieve Willie. His thoughts turned to Emily. He wondered what she was doing; how she was getting along. It seemed like she had been gone for years, although it had only been six weeks or so. He wondered if she missed him as much as he missed her. He thought back to when they first married.

Emily was a beautiful bride! He vividly remembered watching her float gracefully down the aisle like an angel, so beautifully adorned in her grandmother's antique pearl and lace wedding gown. Their wedding day was perfect in every way! They had SO many unfulfilled hopes and dreams ahead of them. Brian was going to enter seminary and seek a doctorate in theology, while Emily wanted to raise a family. How many nights they'd lie awake in bed after the wedding and talk about the plans they had for the future. Emily's face lit up like a Christmas tree when she talked about having children. She was going to make a wonderful mother! She had even started a hope chest of baby clothes in both blue and pink – hoping to have both a boy and a girl – maybe even three or four! And of course, they would stay right there in Shelbyville and raise their family in the beautiful Silver Ridge Mountains!

Brian also hoped to one day have his own church, as well as an outreach ministry for young people – a ministry near and dear to his heart. There were so many lost and confused young people in the world that needed to know about God's merciful grace and all-forgiving love. Having had a rather rebellious youth himself, he knew all too well the dangers and pitfalls a young person encountered as they were growing up. If not for the love, and discipline his own parents had showed him as a young boy, he could have very easily been led astray into the dark world that Satan and his demons offered its young prey. He felt the spirit of the Lord leading him to reach out to young people and help them avoid those treacherous paths of self-destruction. Yes, his and Emily's lives were filled with hopes, dreams, and endless possibilities. Until Baby Jacob died, and Emily left.

How could she throw all that away? What evil stronghold was keeping her at arm's length from her very own husband? And how much longer before he lost her to it forever? The answer scared him and he quickly doused the towering flames of dread with a silent prayer:

Dear Father God, please bless and keep Emily safe wherever she is, and whatever she's doing. Please protect her from Satan's lies and lead her back to the place of love and truth. Lead her back to me, Lord. Please heal her broken heart and help her let go of little Jacob. I need my wife back, Father. And I pray you'll help her realize that she needs me too. Please, God, bring her home soon. Amen.

Brian tossed his empty containers in his lunch bag and walked back toward the front of the shop. "See you tonight around eight!" Karla called out as he was leaving.

"Yea, see you tonight Karla", he called back.

Little did he know that Bible study had been cancelled, due to a broken heat pump in the church that needed to be repaired. It would be as cold in that church as an Alaskan iceberg! Just as Karla had planned. And HER plans for Brian were just as chilling!

CHAPTER 10

*O*nce again, it was Wednesday night, and Pauline and Nellie were busy working on the Christmas pageant costumes, only unbeknownst to Brian, they decided to work at Nellie's house since the furnace was broken in the church. And once again, Brian was left staring at a near-empty refrigerator when he got home from work. *I really need to go grocery shopping soon!* he reminded himself. And there was no time to run down to Rusty's for a burger if he was going to make it to church by eight.

He threw some sliced cheese between two pieces of bread and popped it in the toaster over. Looking back in the fridge, he discovered some of Karla's leftover bean soup hiding in the back. Not exactly a "hungry man meal", but it would have to do. *Maybe they'll have some refreshments there,* he hoped. Emily always provided donuts or homemade cookies, and coffee, when she taught the Bible study. One thing you could count on at Shelbyville Baptist – there was ALWAYS food involved in any church function!

He quickly gobbled down his sandwich and ran upstairs to shower and change clothes, trading in his overhauls and flannel shirt for a pair of khakis and a black pullover sweater. Pulling the sweater down over his chest, he noticed how the ripples in his chest were more defined, and his stomach formed an almost perfectly chiseled six pack. Chopping trees on the Christmas tree farm had definitely whipped him back into shape.

He flexed his rock-hard biceps. They bulged like two pulsating oranges. He clinched his fists, and pumped his muscles up and down a few times. His broad shoulders arched in unison. He stood in front of the dresser mirror and repeated the primal movements, watching with pride as his tight and toned muscles succumbed to his reflexive commands. Still, as big, broad, and strong as he was, his arms were weak and empty without Emily there to hold. He closed his eyes and remembered how good it used to feel to hold her in his arms at night. Her tiny frame fit perfectly in his strong arms and he felt like he could hold her forever. Now the only thing he was holding onto were memories of happier times. And they were quickly fading away with each passing day.

Brian slathered his face with a couple slaps of aftershave lotion and rushed downstairs. As and always, he left the porch light on before leaving for the church.

The parking lot was nearly empty when he arrived at church, with the exception of Karla's Corvette. *Hmm, either I'm early or everyone else is late.* He turned the truck off and quickly slipped in the side door of the church. A light was on in the sanctuary where Bible study was usually held, but there was no sign of any other attendees – or Karla.

"Anybody home?" he called out in the dimmed darkness. Finally Karla appeared from down the hallway.

"Right here, Brian. I was in the kitchen making some coffee." She handed him a Styrofoam cup of steaming java.

"I'm so glad you're here! Doesn't look like anyone else is going to make it tonight, does it? Guess it's just you and me!" she replied, almost sounding relieved. She slurped a big tongue-full of coffee and licked her lips.

"Mmm, this is so good! I don't know WHY it's so cold in here! I turned the heat up but it hasn't come on yet! We might need to pray for the furnace if it doesn't come on soon!" she laughed.

Shelbyville Baptist Church was over a hundred years old, and it had been at least twenty since the heat pump had been replaced. Brian had heard Pauline complaining about how cold the sanctuary was when she came home from church on Sundays. But she always attributed it to the Devil trying to run people "out of the furnace, and into the fire". *Hell's fire*, she'd emphatically reply.

"Have you called Pastor Gray, Karla? Maybe that's the reason no one else is here. Maybe the furnace has finally died. It is quite old, you know, and has been giving the church problems for some time now!" He eyed her suspiciously, as he took another swallow of coffee.

"You know, now that I think about it, I DO seem to remember hearing Pastor Gray say something about the furnace needing some repairs. But I don't think he said anything about it going out, or that Bible study would be cancelled tonight." Another lie. Another scheme. But Brian was onto her. He slid his cell phone from the holster on his pants and quickly punched in Pastor Gray's number.

"Hello, this is Pastor Gray."

"Hey, Pastor, this is Brian Clark."

"Brian, it's good to hear from you; how are you?"

"I'm good Pastor, thanks. Look, I'm here at the church with Karla Beacham for Bible study and the heat won't come on. Is there a problem with that old furnace?"

"Good heavens, yes! Didn't she tell you that it went out last night and the repair man can't get there until Friday?" Brian glanced over at Karla and raised his eyebrows in a stern arch.

"No, she must have forgotten. I'm sorry to have bothered you, Pastor."

"No bother, Brian. Just hate you had to go out in this cold for nothing. You and Karla are welcome to come over here if you'd like to have Bible study with me, though."

"Uh, that's okay, Pastor Gray. We don't want to intrude on your evening. We'll lock up here and be on our way. Besides, I've got an early morning."

"Okay. I understand. Tell your Ma I said hello! Oh, Brian, any word yet from Emily?"

"No, Pastor. Nothing yet. Thanks for asking, though."

"Keep the faith, son, God's doing a work in her, and it might take some time. Just keep the faith."

"Yea, sure, Pastor. I will. Goodnight."

"Night, Brian – be careful going home, you and Karla, too!"

He pushed the OFF button on his phone and slid it back in the holster. Karla had taken a seat on the front row, and was shivering, the bitter cold causing her overly exposed breasts to stand at attention through her plunging V-neckline sweater. Her hands were shaking, and she bounced her knees up and down in a half-concerted effort to stay warm.

"Pastor said the furnace is out. Said he thought you knew." He eyed her again with suspicion and mistrust.

"Oh, yea, you know, NOW I remember, he DID call me yesterday and tell me about that darned furnace. I totally forgot we wouldn't be able to have Bible study tonight! No wonder no one else showed up! He must have called everyone else and told them, too! Ah – ah – ah-choo!" She faked a weak sneeze and a few even weaker sniffles. "I'm SO sorry, Brian!"

Brian knew her sneeze was a fake, just as the lie she'd just told, but offered a friendly *"Bless you!"* anyway. "You better get out of this cold and get home before you catch pneumonia!" he strongly suggested.

"Oh, I'm okay. I just need another cup of coffee." She stood up and brushed by him, laying her hand on his arm. "You know, since we're already here, we may as well have Bible study. Here, let me get you a refill, too" she said brushing her body up against his Besides, you still owe me a Bible challenge, remember!" She slid the now empty cup from his hand.

"Karla, wait, are you crazy?" Karla stopped in her tracks, her back turned toward Brian, waiting for his rebuttal.

"It's about forty degrees in here and getting colder by the minute. If we stay here another ten minutes, we'll BOTH end up with pneumonia. And I'm sure not going to leave your Uncle Roy in a bind like that. He's depending on us too much to run that tree farm! I think we need to leave NOW – both of us!"

Karla turned around and walked in closer to him. As

she got ready to speak, a breath of hot air escaped her mouth and surrounded Brian's face. The chilly air had turned her cheeks and nose a sexy, rosy red and her breasts were still standing at attention underneath her tight, body-clinging sweater.

"Won't you stay and have just one more cup of coffee with me, Brian? I really need someone to talk to tonight" she begged. She lowered her big doleful eyes, batted her dark lashes, and blew another breath of hot air in his face in a torrid attempt to persuade him to stay. This woman was a skillful hunter, her claws fully sharpened and ready to strike! He felt like he was trapped in a cage with a wild animal. He knew he should leave right then. But his feet felt like steel weights, his body already frozen in place. *The mind is willing, but the flesh is weak....*

He stepped back and put his hands in his coat pockets.

"No, Karla, I'm sorry, I can't. Not tonight. We can talk Friday when I come over for dinner. We really should be getting out of here before we catch our death of cold."

Karla rolled her eyes and sighed in defeated disgust. She tossed the empty cups in a nearby trashcan and grabbed her Bible and purse.

"Sure Brian, whatever you say."

She bolted ahead of him and flipped the light switch behind her, purposely leaving him in total darkness He followed blindly behind, making his way to the door locking and shutting it tightly behind him. Before he could even get in his truck, Karla was already backing up and heading out of the parking lot, screeching tires behind her. Brian got in his truck, turned the ignition, and flipped the heat up to high. He rubbed his numb hands briskly between his knees trying to warm them up. He thought about Karla's ill-devised scheme, and how she had gone to such great lengths to get his attention. Ironically, if she hadn't been so deceptive, he might have stayed and at least PRAYED for her wayward soul! God knows someone needed to pray for that girl! But he was dealing with WAY too much right now to play her silly games.

Sorry, Karla, he sighed as he put the truck in reverse. *Ma warned me about you and she was right! But I WILL set you straight Friday night! That's all I need - is for Emily to come home and find out another woman has been stalking me!*

Safely back at home, Karla Beacham pulled a piece of paper from her purse, picked up her cell phone, and dialed the number written on the paper. After two rings, a young woman answered.

"Hello, is this Emily Clark? Emily, this is Karla Beacham in Shelbyville. You don't know me, but there's something I think you should know about your husband"…

CHAPTER 11

*O*ld man Collin's rooster next door woke Brian up bright, and early the next morning, along with the thawing rays of another winter's sun. December had come in unusually cold this year, even for the usually snow-capped mountains that lined the sleepy village of Shelbyville. Still, brisk cold weather was a Christmas tree farmer's best friend, as it beckoned shoppers with a jolly spirit and enticed early Christmas tree shopping.

Waking up a little earlier than usual, thanks to an insomniac rooster, Brian savored a blissfully long and hot shower, then scurried downstairs for a cup of coffee with Pauline before he headed to work. He could already smell the nutty wheat aroma of banana nut muffins drifting quickly upstairs.

"Mmm, that smell is gonna cause the bears to come down out of the mountains!" Brian mused as he walked up behind Pauline and kissed her on the cheek.

"I don't know about that, but there DOES seem to be another wild animal stalking a certain person around here...".She turned around, arched her eyebrows, and gave Brian *"the look"*.

"What's that supposed to mean, Ma?" he questioned, fearing she knew about Karla's Bible study caper the night before.

"Whose bright idea was it to call a Bible study meeting last night, knowing the furnace was broken? And who was dumb enough to go, when everyone else knew the meeting had been cancelled?"

"How'd you find out about that?" Brian asked, his fears about Karla's scheme quickly coming to light.

"Pastor Gray called me to see if you and Karla made it

home alright. He was "concerned" about you." Brian poured a cup of coffee and sat down at the table. He drummed his fingers nervously against his cup.

"Ma, don't start again. She said she forgot about the broken furnace. We had a cup of coffee and then left. There's no reason to make anything more out of it."

"FORGOT??! Brian, son, I hope I raised you with more sense than THAT! Do you REALLY believe Karla forgot that the church was going to be empty AND cold last night? Give the girl credit – she knew EXACTLY what she was doing!" She slid a plate with a hot, steaming muffin in front of him. The steam reminded him of Karla's hot, smoking lies. He already felt like a fool for even agreeing to meet her there, and kicked himself for it repeatedly when he got home. Now Pauline was on him about it.

"MA, STOP IT! I told you before that I can handle a woman like Karla Beacham. Now just let it be! She is NOT scheming on me and even if she were, she's wasting her time! You know my heart belongs to Emily. And SHE knows it too! We've talked a little about things and she knows I'm NOT interested in any other woman besides my WIFE!" He took a bite out of his muffin and washed it down with some coffee. Pauline kept silent, but was still not certain Brian realized how dangerous Karla Beacham really was.

"Your lunch is in the fridge. Leftover turkey and dressing from Nellie. See you tonight," Pauline said as she opened the back door to leave.

"Wait, Ma" Brian looked up at her with apologetic eyes. "Thanks, and tell Ms. Nellie I said thanks, too." Pauline smiled back, but Brian could see the worry and concern she hid behind her bifocals. He got up, walked over, and kissed her on the cheek.

"Don't worry, Ma; I got it all under control – I promise." Pauline cupped his cheek in her hand for just a second – this grown, handsome young man who would always be her sensitive and loving, yet naïve, little boy. How she feared he was in for even more heartbreak to come with Karla Beacham around!

"I hope so, son; I hope so" she replied as she walked out the door.

Brian took another hefty bite of his muffin and slurped down the rest of his coffee. He glanced at the clock on the wall. He still had plenty of time before he was due into work, but decided he would go ahead in and get things straight with Karla first thing. *Lord, you know my heart belongs to Emily. Help me make Karla understand that so she'll stop coming onto me. And Lord, help her find a good man to share her life with. Amen.*

His thoughts turned again to Emily. He stared up at the calendar. Tomorrow would make seven weeks since she'd been gone. It seemed like it had been seven years. How much longer was she going to make him wait? Or was she EVEN coming to come back at all? *This is crazy. There's no way we're ever going to work this out with us apart like this. I think I'll just head on up to Cherokee Hills Saturday morning and surprise her. Maybe I can convince her to come home. At least I can try.*

Glad to have a plan in place to bring his wife home, he jumped in the truck and headed to the tree farm. It would be a long day, but thoughts of soon reuniting with his beautiful Emily made him smile, and would help get him through the day. In the meantime, he needed to set the record straight with a certain sneaky seductress named Karla!

"**K**arla, we need to talk" Brian announced as he barged in the Christmas shop fifteen minutes later.

"Sure, Brian, what's up? Wanna cup of hot apple cider?" She left him standing at the front while she trotted off to the back. Brian followed quickly behind.

"No, thanks, but listen...."

"Look, Brian", Karla interrupted, "Before you say anything, I just want to apologize for dragging you out in the cold last night to the church. I can't believe I completely forgot about that furnace thing!" She shook her head in self-disgust as she poured a cup of hot cider.

"And I want to apologize for leaving so abruptly. I was just disappointed that you didn't want to stay and talk with me. I was just feeling kind of sad, you know, missing my mom and all. But that was no excuse to be rude to you and I'm sorry. Still friends?" She cast him a remorseful look, and held out her free hand in return for a handshake. Brian blew out a defeated sigh and reluctantly shook her hand.

"Sure, Karla. Still friends. But look, you still need to understand something..." Brrrrinnnnng! Brrrinnnng! This time, the shop phone interrupted him.

"Oh, excuse me, Brian, I need to get that! We'll talk later, 'kay?" Karla scurried back up to the front to answer the phone, leaving Brian with a mouthful of unfinished words.

With Karla yakking nonstop on the phone, and customers starting to stream in, he gave up on talking to her. At least for the moment. But he was determined to set that girl straight – before Pauline did it for him!

After another long nine hour shift, only stopping twenty minutes for a quick lunch, Brian called it a day. Karla had been busy as well with Christmas shop customers all day so Brian never got another chance to talk to her. It was just as well. He felt like he had a chain saw permanently attached to his hand, and every muscle in his body cried out for a long hot soak in a hot tub. Not to mention he was dirty, sweaty, and exhausted.

He stopped at Rusty's on the way home and grabbed a Burger Deal, figuring Pauline would once again "be about the Lord's business" mending Christmas costumes. Just as well. Besides a quick supper and a long hot bath, there was nothing more he wanted than to lay down and sleep. Tomorrow was Friday and Roy was due back Saturday. He would finally get a much-needed weekend off - not to mention a trip to Cherokee Hills to see Emily.

As he drove home, he dreamed about seeing his

beautiful angel again. He couldn't wait to hold her in his arms and feel her baby-soft skin next to his. How he longed to smell the freshness of her hair, and the delicate sweet scent of her perfume. He missed the soft, sexiness of her voice – the way she used to say *"I love you, baby"*. Her smile. Her laugh. The way she walked across the room. He missed everything about her. Most of all, he missed making love to his wife.

Emily was a wonderful lover – kind, attentive, and eager to please. He used to tease her by telling her when they made love, he felt like he was at the "top of a mountain". *"You ARE on a mountaintop, silly"* she'd tease back. When they made love, time stood still and they both basked in the afterglow of love that was as perfect as Heaven above! No woman had ever made him feel so complete – or so manly. How he missed the tender affections of a loving woman!

As he pulled in the drive, he noticed a large crate on the front porch. He jumped out of the truck and walked up to the porch. An invoice was attached to the top that read: *Heaven On Earth Memorials.* Baby Jacobs memorial stone had arrived by express service! What perfect timing! Now he had another reason to go see Emily. She would want to know about the memorial stone. Maybe THAT would entice her to come home, so they could put it on Baby Jacob's grave together. Maybe it would be the closure they both needed to let go, and finally move on with their lives. God's timing seemed impeccable and Brian felt like an angel was sitting on his shoulder. He looked up to the canvass of stars spread out above him and thanked God for the hope that lied ahead. A hope and a future, just as He had promised in His word.

He walked inside, and as he guessed, Pauline was gone. He took his fast food supper in the den, plopped down in his recliner and turned on the TV to catch the evening news. The weather report had just started. *"A strong snowstorm is moving in from the west with the potential for heavy snow beginning Friday afternoon into the weekend,"* the weatherman reported with stark certainty.

"Oh great, that's just what I need – a snowstorm!" Brian muttered to himself. Didn't matter. Mountain people were used to heavy snow in the winter. It was practically a way of life from November to March. Snow tires and chains were "standard equipment" on everyone's vehicles in Shelbyville, lest you ended up stranded at the bottom of the mountain! And although driving in a snowstorm would be a pain, NOTHING was going to keep him from going to Cherokee Hills on Saturday to see his sweet Emily. Nothing – not even a foot or two of snow!

With sleep bearing down on his weary eyes, he struggled to stay awake to watch the rest of the news, so he finally went up to take a shower. After his bath, he snuggled down deep in the flannel sheets of his bed, and with tender thoughts of Emily rolling over softly in his mind, and a dose of Extra Strength Tylenol slowly kicking in; he finally drifted off to a restful sleep.

Meanwhile, Karla Beacham was doing a little planning of her own...

CHAPTER 12

*W*ith the threat of a winter storm coming, there were already early customers swarming around the tree farm when Brian arrived for work the next day. He and Willie had sawed and loaded twelve trees before ten o'clock before they got their first morning break. Karla, too, had a steady stream of customers in and out of the Christmas shop, and had already run out of Sally's homemade granny-apple butter, scuppernong grape jelly and honey-bee molasses. Luckily, Roy had more stored in the cellar at his house, just across the road. Karla took advantage of a midmorning lull in customers and ran over to restock her supply, while Brian kept an eye on things at the store. He welcomed the much-needed break, and took the opportunity to catch up on the weather report while Karla was gone.

"*Looks like the snowstorm is moving faster, and will arrive much earlier than we thought*", the weatherman drearily reported.

"Please, Lord, give me a break! Can't you hold off on the white stuff 'til I get to Cherokee Hills? Then you can let it snow ten feet deep for all I care!" Brian muttered under his breath. Unless he beat the snow there, it would be too hazardous to drive in it at night –even with snow tires and chains. And as busy as the day had already been, there was no way he was going to be able to cut out early and leave. He could only hope God would honor his prayer and save the snow for Christmas Day!

"Hey Brian, can you help me unload all this stuff from my car?" Karla asked, interrupting Brian's wishful prayer when she returned. "Sure, Karla" he said following her back outside.

"Wow, look at you!" she bragged as Brian lifted two heavy cases of homemade goods in jars from her trunk. "Sure

would be nice to have muscles like THAT around MY house!"
she exclaimed, poking at the hard bulges that popped up
through Brian's thermal shirt. He ignored her flattery and
quickly carried the cases inside, then returned to her car to
retrieve the rest. He had to admit though, it felt nice to have
someone notice his well-defined biceps – courtesy of his last
couple of weeks playing lumberjack. Feeling a little more
cocky, he lifted the remaining three cases, balanced them on
his left shoulder, and strutted past Karla like a proud peacock.
Karla shot him a sexy wink, and followed along behind him
into the shop.

"Just put them behind the counter – I've got to price
them before I put them on the shelves. And thank you SO
much, Brian! Wish I could have taken you with me to go get
them! I nearly broke three fingernails loading those darn
boxes in my trunk!" She waved her hand in front of him and
giggled.

"Oh, by the way, don't forget we have a date tonight –
uh, I mean – you're still coming over for my homemade pizza
right?" Brian winced, knowing her slip up on words was quite
intentional.

"Yea, about that, Karla. I don't think I can make it after
all. You see, I'm heading out to Cherokee Hills tonight. Going
to see my wife. She's been staying there with her mom for a
few weeks, trying to sort things out, and I feel like I need to be
there with her, you know?" Karla arched her eyebrows and
Brian could tell the wheels of deception were spinning fast.

"Oh, well, sure, Brian – I can understand that. But if I
were you, I wouldn't leave tonight – there's a big snowstorm
coming and it's going to be MUCH too dangerous to be
driving! Why don't you wait and leave tomorrow when its
daylight? I'm sure it would be much safer traveling during the
day, don't you think?"

Karla started unpacking the jars, deliberately bending
over in front of Brian, her tight black denim jeans accentuating
her hourglass figure. Brian felt a hot glow come over his

cheeks and travel down to his loins. Like a speeding bullet, testosterone surged through his body. Moreover, the enemy was shooting deadly arrows of temptation in every direction as Karla sashayed in front, and around him; circling him like a buzzard circling its dead prey. He felt the sweat bead up on his forward and the sticky perspiration form under his armpits. What WAS it about this woman that melted ALL his resolve and conviction?

"I don't know, Karla. I'm just going to see how the weather goes and play it by ear. I'm definitely not going to do anything foolish like driving in a blizzard, but if at all possible, I WILL be leaving as soon as the roads are safe to drive! I'm afraid I'll have to take a rain check on that pizza – or "snow-check", if you don't mind!" He coughed up a dry laugh and waited for her rebuttal. However, much to his surprise, she backed down and gave up quite easily. TOO easy, in fact!

"I understand, Brian. I hope you're able to go see your wife. I really do. But please, don't put yourself in harm's way. She's already lost a son – I'd hate for her to lose a husband, too." Her concern seemed ALMOST genuine, but there was something in her voice, that argued otherwise.

With more customers piling in, Brian went back out to the lot, while Karla started tagging the jars. The "date" seemed cancelled for now, but Brian wasn't so sure she was going to give up THAT easy!

Around four o'clock, business once again slowed down and Brian headed to the shop to get a cup of coffee and a slice of warm apple cake that Mrs. Shepherd, a long time customer of Roy's, had given him earlier. He figured he'd share it with Karla – kind of a "peace offering" for skipping out on her pizza invitation that night. Smiling and whistling, he opened the door to the shop and called out to Karla. Usually she was right behind the counter, but he didn't see her there.

"Hey Karla, where are you?" he yelled to the back. Suddenly, he heard a low moaning coming from behind the counter.

"Brian, I'm here – on the floor. Please, help me!" Brian rushed around the counter and saw Karla lying curled up in a fetal position on the floor.

"Good Lord, Karla, what happened? Are you alright?"

"Oh, Brian, thank goodness you came in! I fell from the ladder while I was putting up those jars, and I think I broke my ankle!" She grabbed at her left leg and moaned pitifully again in pain.

"Here, let's see if we can get you up", Brian said, trying to pull Karla to her feet. But she resisted his help and just kept moaning and groaning. "No, I can't, it hurts too bad! Please, don't make me stand up! Can you just carry me over to the table?" Like a toddler reaching out for its mother, she grabbed for Brian's arms and quickly threw hers around his neck. Brian scooped her up in his massive arms and toted her back to the picnic table in back, then set her down on the bench.

"I better call an ambulance. If your leg is broken, you might need surgery." He reached for his cell phone but Karla stopped him before he could dial 911.

"No, wait. Don't call. I don't really think it's broken; more like sprained. Let me just sit here for a minute and see if the pain eases up." Brian returned his cell phone to its holster and sat down beside her.

"Is your ankle swollen?" he asked half-heartedly.

"I don't know – could you untie my shoe so we can check?" She peered up at him, forcing two big tears in her eyes. Brian carefully lifted her left leg onto his lap and untied her granny-style ankle boot, then slid it slowly off her foot. He slid her sock down over her ankle and inspected her foot for any sign of swelling. He gently squeezed her ankle and then tapped around the bottom of her foot.

"Oww", she groaned, and pulled her foot away. "That hurts, Brian. I think it's swollen some too, don't you?" Brian grabbed her foot back and poked at it again. It did feel somewhat puffy and swollen, but was definitely NOT broken.

"Can you rotate your foot around or side to side? Karla slowly moved her foot from right to left, then made a half circle with her big toe, moaning lowly the whole time.

"Yes, but it hurts to do that. I really think I sprained my ankle. I've done the same thing before playing tennis in college and it felt exactly the same way. I just need to get off my feet and rest for a couple of days. I'm sure I'll be alright."

"Are you sure you don't want me to call a doctor, or someone to come pick you up? Is there anyone who can come get you and take you home?"

"No, I really don't have anyone." She poked her lips out like a pouting child and cast her head down pitifully; hoping Brian would take the bait. Much to her content, he did – hook, line and sinker!

"Then I'll take you home. Just let me help Willie finish up til Ed and Sara get here, then we'll leave. I'll put the CLOSED sign on the door and lock the shop. Willie and I can collect the money from the customers outside. Here, you go lie down back here and rest til I get back."

He once again scooped her up in his arms, carried her to the back room, and laid her down on the single bed Roy had put back there. She smiled with great satisfaction, went limp in his arms, and relished in his kind attentions.

"This is really very sweet of you, Brian. I really appreciate it" she sweetly whispered in his ear as he laid her down. "Do you think you could get me some Tylenol behind the counter before you leave? My ankle is sort of aching now."

"Sure thing. I'll be right back. A few minutes later, he returned with two Tylenol and a bottle of water.

"Here, take these and try to rest. I'll be back in about an hour." Karla swallowed the pills and took a couple swigs of water. Pitifully, she lay back on the bed and weakly moaned. *She should have been an actress*, Brian thought. Still, it was obvious she was in pain, and despite her devious plans, he couldn't just ignore her. After all, didn't the Bible say, ***"But whoso hath this world's good, and seeth his brother have need, and*** *shutteth up his bowels of compassion from him, how dwelleth the love of God in him?"* (1 John 3:17 KJV)

Brian put the CLOSED sign on the Christmas shop door, and pulled the door to behind him. Back outside, a brisk snow had started to fall and was quickly covering the ground. He looked up at the dimpled, graying skies. "Thanks a lot, God", he disgustedly muttered as he headed back to the tree lot. If it kept up, the snow would pile up too quickly for him to drive safely to Shelbyville. Not to mention he had to take Karla home before he left. Looked like he was in for TWO snow jobs in the same day!

As the snow fell faster, business quickly slowed down, customers opting to make last minute trips to the grocery store instead. Brian was at least thankful for that. Maybe he could get Karla safely home, and still head to Shelbyville before the roads got too bad. Ed, Sara and Chad showed up around five, but they all decided to close the tree lot in view of the threatening winter storm approaching. Brian hurried back to the Christmas shop and found Karla asleep in the back where he had left her an hour earlier.

"Karla..., wake up.... it's me, Brian! Get up – we've got to go – its snowing really hard and we need to get you home!" Karla groggily lifted her eyelids and groaned. She reached up with both arms toward Brian's neck.

"I don't think I can walk, Brian. Can you carry me?" she moaned. He had halfway expected her response and once again scooped her up in his arms. She went limp like a rag doll and nestled in his chest as he carried her out to the truck.

"Oh, I forgot my coat and purse –Can you get them for me, please?" Brian hurried back to the shop, retrieved her coat and purse, and returned to the truck.

"Here, you should put this on" he instructed, tossing the coat to her. It'll take a few minutes for the truck to warm up." Shaking and chattering her teeth, Karla threw her coat on and slid over closer to Brian.

"It's fr-fr-fr-freezing!" she whined. Brian put the truck in drive and slowly pulled out. The snow was now coming down in blinding sheets and the wind was causing snow drifts to pile up alongside the road. Another hour and the roads would be impassable to drive at night. It looked like he wouldn't make to Shelbyville anytime soon! Fortunately, Karla only lived a few miles down the road. Hopefully, he could get her settled in and get home himself before it got too rough.

With Karla still burrowing close beside him, he finagled his cell phone from his side and called Pauline.

"Hey, Ma, it's me. You home?"

"Yes, son, but where are YOU?"

"Good" he said, ignoring her question. "Stay put. Looks like this is going to be a bad storm. I'm on the way to take Karla home. She fell at the shop and sprained her ankle so I gotta drive her home. As soon as I get her settled in, I'm heading home."

"Oh really? Well, now, poor thing. Wasn't she lucky that she had YOU to play Prince Charming for her?" Brian switched the phone to his other ear so Karla couldn't hear Pauline's snide remarks.

"It's okay, Ma. She's going to be fine. I'll be home soon as I can. Love you, bye!" He returned his phone to his side and flipped the heat switch up to HIGH.

"Are you getting warm now, Karla?" Brian asked.

"Yea, I am now," she replied, snuggling up close beside him. "Thanks again for bringing me home. I could have NEVER driven home in this mess – and certainly not with a messed up ankle! Guess you're my Good Samaritan, huh?"

"Yea, I guess" Brian answered weakly. Her comment triggered the story of the real Good Samaritan in the Bible:

"Which now of these three, thinkest thou, was neighbour unto him that fell among the thieves? And he said, He that shewed mercy on him. Then said Jesus unto him, Go, and do thou

likewise." (Luke 10:36-37 KJV)

That's exactly what Brian had done– had mercy on Karla at a time when she was hurt and weak. Why then, did God not answer his prayer about the snow? Didn't He know Brian needed to be with Emily – NOT Karla? Besides, Karla had not been honest with Brian all week. She was scheming, conniving and untrustworthy. Still, Brian felt God leading him to be nice to her. But why?

They finally pulled into Karla's drive, and Brian drove directly across the yard and right up to the front door, figuring it would be easier to tote her in, the closer he was to the door. With the winds furiously snapping and the snow flying wildly through the air, he ran around to the other side of the truck and carefully lifted Karla out, and into his arms.

"Where's the key to the door?" he yelled through the howling winds.

"Here – on my purse." He grabbed the key ring she had attached to the metal ring on her purse. "It's the big round head key", she instructed. He threw her over his back, and jangled the key ring around until he found the house key, then unlocked the door.

"Whew, that's a wicked wind" he remarked, slamming the door behind him. "Here, let me help you down here on the couch." He gently laid her down on the couch and brushed the snow from her hair and clothes.

"Brr! It's cold in here! Could you turn the heat up for me, Brian? The thermostat's in the hall, there." Brian made his way down the darkened hall and bumped up the heat. Karla's parents had restored the old home place some years ago and thankfully had replaced the old furnace with a new updated gas pack. Soon, the warm whirring of gas heat was circulating up through the vents. Brian shed his wet boots by the door and hung his coat up on the rack by the entryway, then returned to the living room where Karla was.

"Can I fix you something to eat or drink, Karla?" he asked, still remembering the story of the Good Samaritan, who had gone the extra mile for the unfortunate soul who had been beaten and robbed.

"Well, I AM kind of hungry. How about that pizza we were going to fix? I've got all the makings in the kitchen – if you want, we could fix it together. Besides, it's much too bad outside for you to leave right now! Why don't you stay a while and wait for the snow to let up?" It had been a long, hard day for Brian. He eased back in the chair beside the couch. Karla's house was getting warm and toasty, and the idea of fresh homemade pizza was sounding better and better. *I suppose it wouldn't hurt for me to stay a little while – just in case she needed anything, or got to feeling worse. Besides, there's no way I'll ever be able to drive to Cherokee Hills tonight. Best if I get a fresh start tomorrow,* he reasoned.

"Well, I guess I could stay a little while longer. I'd hate for you to have to cook standing up on one foot!" he laughed. "Point me to the kitchen and I'll try my hand at that pizza you were talking about!"

"Great! If you'll help me up, I think I can hobble back there with you and give you a hand!" she replied. Brian helped her up and slowly they made their way to the big country kitchen in the back of the house.

"Just help me over to the table and I'll prop my leg up on a chair." Karla instructed.

"There you go" Brian said, easing her down, just before his cell phone went to ringing. It was Pauline.

"Brian, son, where in the world are you? There's already four inches of snow on the ground! Did you get Karla home okay? Ya'll are not stranded somewhere are you?"

"No, Ma, we're fine. I'm here with her now at her house. I'm going to stay a little while and fix her something to eat, and then I'll be on my way home."

"Do you think that's wise, son? I mean, can't she open a can of soup or something without YOUR help?" she said sarcastically. Brian walked into the hall, out of Karla's earshot.

"Ma, I'm just being a Good Samaritan – like you taught

me, remember? I'll be home after a while – don't worry – I'll be careful driving home!"

"It's not the drive home later I'm worried about, Brian - it's the snow job that girls' putting over on you NOW!"

"Stop it, Ma! Karla sprained her ankle and she can barely walk! What kind of person would I be if I just abandoned her here? She doesn't know anyone else in Shelbyville and Roy's not due home 'til tomorrow! This is his niece for God's sake – what kind of friend would I be if I didn't take care of her? Now please, stop making problems where none exists! I'll call you as soon as I head home!"

Without waiting for Pauline's next comment, he ended the call. It was the first time he could ever remember hanging up on his Moma. But she just would NOT let it go about Karla! Besides, Brian still felt led to be a friend to Karla. Call it "preacher's intuition", but he felt as if there were some reason God kept throwing them together. Maybe he could help Karla understand why she felt the need to lie and try to manipulate others. Or maybe it was a test – to see if he had what it takes to be a minister. Or maybe God was using him to witness to Karla. Whatever the reason, he had to be obedient and heed the call. In time, Pauline would see that he did the right thing.

"Everything okay with Pauline?" Karla asked as Brian returned to the kitchen.

"Uh, yea, sure; she's just worried that I'm out in this snowstorm. You know how mothers are!" Karla looked down and tearfully sighed.

"Oh, I'm sorry, Karla. I forgot you just recently lost your mom. I'm really sorry – that was an insensitive thing to say - I didn't mean to upset you." He reached over and put his arm on her shoulder.

"Hey, look, let's make that pizza! I'm starving!" Karla looked up through big crocodile tears and smiled back, again pleased that Brian was playing right into her act.

"Okay, me too. The pizza stone is in the cabinet over there, and the pizza dough and fixings are in the fridge. Let's make a pizza!"

As Brian got everything out of the refrigerator for the pizza, Karla sat back smugly in her chair and watched with a satisfied look of delight. *Mission accomplished.* He had bought the whole sprained ankle scheme - hook, line and sinker! Time now to reel in her catch!

Meanwhile, upstairs, her bed was warm and waiting...

CHAPTER 13

"*M*mm...that pizza smells heavenly, Brian! An Italian Lumberjack! What more could a girl want?" she flirtatiously teased. Brian lifted the hot, steaming pizza from the oven and set the stone on the wooden island bar to cool. He had to admit, Karla's homemade pasta sauce was bold and flavorful – the perfect compliment to the stringy mozzarella cheese and fresh cut toppings!

"You know, I think I'd like a glass of wine with my pizza. How about you, Brian?" Karla pointed over to a wine bar in the corner of the kitchen.

"Oh, I'm not much on wine; but I'll take a beer if you've got one" he replied as he walked over to the wine bar and poured Karla a glass of red wine.

"Sure – there's some beer in the fridge. Help yourself!" It had been a long time since Brian had imbibed in ANY kind of alcohol, but he remembered how good a cold beer tasted with pizza! *One can't hurt anything*, he reasoned as he grabbed a cold one from the fridge and popped off the top.

"How's your ankle?" Brian asked as he served both of them a generous slice of pizza.

"Oh, it's okay, but it's still sore and achy. I'm sure it will be fine in a few days. The wine seems to be helping the pain, though – how about pour me another glass?" Brian hesitated, but figured the more relaxed she was, the sooner she would go to sleep and he could leave.

"And have yourself another beer!" she suggested, as he walked over to the wine bar.

Why not? Still got half a pizza to wash down, Brian thought, grabbing another beer from the fridge. He looked up at the clock on the stove – it was only seven-thirty.

"Hey, Karla, mind if I turn on the TV and check the

weather report?" he asked as he returned with her wine.

"Help yourself," she answered. Brian flipped on the TV remote to the 36" flat screen TV that was mounted above the wine bar, and tuned it to the weather channel. As they munched on the cooled pizza, they listened to the latest weather update.

"They've already got four inches in Shelbyville and the snow seems to be falling fast and furious. Expect another one to two inches by morning, then some clearing tomorrow afternoon. If you're in Shelbyville, you might want to hunker down by a warm fire and put in a good movie – it's going to be a long, cold and snowy night!" the meteorologist reported.

Brian got up and looked out the window. He could barely see the tires on his truck. The snow was quickly piling up! There was no way he was going to make it to Cherokee Hills, but he did need to be getting home!

"Well, I guess I should be going, Karla, before I get snowed in" he said, quickly finishing his pizza and chugging the last swallow of his beer. "Can I do anything for you before I leave?"

Karla poked out her lower lip just slightly and looked up at Brian with sad hound-dog eyes. She looked just like Jesse's old hunting hounds after a hard day of running deer! He laughed to himself and prepared for her calculated stalls.

"Yea, I guess you better; but I REALLY hate to see you try to drive home in this mess!" she replied with a worried tone.

"Oh, its no big deal – I've got the best snow tires Michelin makes on that old truck – they'll get me home safely!" He chunked the empty beer can into the trash, then yawned and stretched his arms up to the ceiling. Karla couldn't help but drool over his broad shoulders and strong arms as he stretched like a waking cat. She remembered how easily he had toted her in his muscular arms into the house, and how safe and protected she felt in his embrace. What she wouldn't give to have those same arms around her all night long! And how could she forget her dreamy fantasy at the top of his stairs the other night?

"Well, I guess you know best, but I'd feel just awful if something happened to you on the way home! You know, Brian, you're welcome to stay right here tonight – you know this old house has PLENTY of room! Why don't you just call Pauline and tell her you're going to stay here? I'm sure she wouldn't want you driving out in this storm, either!"

Oh, now, wouldn't THAT go over just great with Ma? -me spending the night here with Karla Beacham? Why, if I even dared SUGGEST such a thing, she'd damn me to hell up one side and down the other! The thought was so ridiculous, it was almost funny! He looked out the window again. The snow had let up a little, but was still coming down hard. If he didn't leave now, he'd certainly be forced to stay – whether he wanted to or not.

"No, Karla, I need to go now before it gets any worse. Think you'll be okay now? Want me to help you to the couch?" Karla again put on her best pathetic look - the couch not exactly being what she had in mind!

"Well, if you're leaving, I'd just as soon go on up to bed. Could you help me up the stairs?" she begged.

"Are you sure you don't want to sleep down here, tonight Karla? Wouldn't it be easier to get around better downstairs?" he replied, not sure he trusted her within ten feet of a bedroom!

"Oh, no, I don't sleep very well on the couch – I'll sleep much better in my own bed. If you could just help me up the stairs, I think I'll be okay. My ankle is feeling pretty good right now – thanks to the wine! I'll just pop a couple of ibuprofen and sleep like a baby!"

"Well, okay, if you're sure" he reluctantly agreed. Helping Karla to her feet, and leaning on him for support, she hobbled alongside him, as they slowly made their way up each stair step, finally reaching the top of the stairs.

"My room is this way", she pointed, leading Brian

straight to her bedroom. But just before they got to the bedroom door, Karla froze and cried out in pain.

"Oww! Oh my God!" she groaned. Her whole body went limp and she slumped against Brian's chest.

"What? What is it, Karla – what's wrong?"

"My ankle – oh God, a sharp, shooting pain just went through it! Oh, it hurts so baaaad! Can you carry me to the bed, Brian – pleaaaase?"

Brian lifted Karla up in his arms, with hers wrapped tightly around his neck, and toted her into the bedroom. He gently lowered her down onto the California king sized bed, but instead of letting go, she pulled him down closer, until he was just about atop her.

"Oh, Brian, baby, please, lay with me. Please don't leave me now – please – stay with me until I fall asleep." Then she reached up and boldly kissed him on the lips. Her lips were soft and moist; her tongue eager to explore. Between the intoxicating effects of the beer, and Karla's warm breath on his lips, Brian was helpless to resist the temptation.

He slowly sank down into the bed and slid next to her, his body suddenly yearning for more of hers. She pulled him closer – her lips wildly reaching out to his. And although the temperature outside was a frigid thirty degrees, Karla's bedroom was quickly heating up with burning passion between the two star-crossed lovers. The moment she had schemed for was finally within her grasp. She was about to become Brian Clark's mistress!

Suddenly, the light on his cell phone lit up the room like an exploding star. The tune of "Amazing Grace" followed. He jerked up, as if he had been hit with a bolt of lightning. Big beads of perspiration trailed down his face, cascaded around his nose, and dripped down, salting the corners of his parched lips. He grabbed the phone from his side, which was still playing his favorite hymn, and looked at the caller ID. It was Pauline. It was then he realized just how in control God was of his life! Two seconds later and he might have done an unspeakable act. His phone quit ringing. A few seconds later, his voicemail alert chimed. Pauline had left a message.

"Brian, baby, its okay. Whoever it was, you can call them back," Karla whispered in his ear. She put her arms around his neck and tried to pull him back down. However, he resisted her coaxing and pulled away.

"NO! I can't do this, Karla. I WON'T do this! I have to go – this was a mistake – a BIG mistake!"

He bounced up from her bed and stormed clumsily out of the bedroom. As he passed a hall bath, he rushed in, slammed the door behind him, and turned the cold water faucet wide open. He splashed his face repeatedly with icy, cold water, trying to wash away the horrid guilt that was pulsing through his veins. A sickening nausea stewed in the pit of his stomach. He collapsed to his knees; just barely making it to the nearby toilet before a flood of vomit came spewing from his mouth. He hung his head over the toilet, drained and weak, a combination of too much beer and not enough spiritual discipline. He took a towel from the rack above and wiped his face. Cold, icy chills set in as he thought about what just almost happened. *How could I have done this to Emily? After all she's been through, how could I have let this happen?*

"Brian, honey… 'you alright in there?" Karla asked, tapping lightly on the bathroom door. Brian unlocked the door and slowly opened it to find Karla standing there in just a long low-cut nightshirt, her injured ankle "miraculously healed!" He glared menacingly at her, and brushed quickly past her, making a beeline for the door.

"Brian, wait… where are you going? Please don't leave – we need to talk!" she called out, quickly trailing behind him down the stairs.

"I have to go, Karla – I shouldn't have come – we'll talk later!" he answered, quickly putting his boots on and rushing out the front door. He trudged through the deepening snow to his truck and quickly jumped in. His truck stalled as he turned the ignition several times, but finally started. He revved the motor a few times and flipped on the heat switch. Once again, his cell phone erupted with "Amazing Grace". And once again, it was Pauline.

"Yea, Ma, what's up?" he answered casually, hoping his guilty conscience wouldn't give him away.

"Brian, where in God's name are you? Please don't tell me you're still at that Jezebel's house!"

"No, Ma, I'm not", he lied. "I just ran to Rusty's to get a bite to eat and ran into some old friends I hadn't seen lately. Time just got away from me, but I'm heading home now."

"Well, be careful, son – it's already a half of foot of snow in the yard, but I think the snow plows are still clearing the main road. Please take your time and drive safe!"

"I will, Ma. Don't worry. And Ma?"

"Yea, son?"

"Say a prayer for me, will ya?"

"Always, son, I'm ALWAYS praying for you!" she replied, detecting a worried tone in his voice.

With tears stinging his rosy, frostbitten cheeks, Brian put the truck into drive and pulled out onto the snowy, treacherous road, trading one dangerous situation for another…

CHAPTER 14

*W*hat should have been only a fifteen-minute ride home, ended up taking thirty, but Brian finally made it home safe and sound. Thankfully, the snow had stopped and there was no more mention of any in the forecast. With any luck, the roads would be drivable in a couple of days and he could still make the trip to go see Emily.

As he trudged through the heaped snow to the front porch, he noticed Pauline's light on from the side of the house. No doubt she was up, waiting to make sure he got home safely. He knew he'd be in for one hell of a lecture, but for some reason he needed to be with his Moma. Carefully backtracking, he trudged around the side of the house toward Pauline's cozy little cabin nestled closely behind his. As he approached the front, she opened the front door and met him on the porch.

"Thank God you made it home safely, son! What in the world were you thinking staying out in this storm like that? Don't you know I was worried sick?" She barely gave him time to lick the wounds from that tongue-lashing before she started in again.

"I told you NOT to go over there to that girl's house! Can't you see what she's after? For God's sake, Brian, even though you and Emily are separated right now, you're STILL a married man! What would people say if they knew you went traipsing over to that Jezebel's house at night?"

Ma continued her tirade while Brian shed his wet, snow-covered boots on the porch. "And just who were these "old friends" you said you met up with at Rusty's? When I come by there earlier, it looked like he had already closed for the evening! Where were you REALLY, Brian? Still over at Karla Beacham's house? Please tell me you didn't DO anything with that girl!"

"Enough, Ma!" Brian shouted. "That's enough!" He had heard just about all he could take and then some. Pauline stepped away and cut him a glaring eye. "I'll get you some supper", she mumbled as she started to walk off toward the kitchen.

"Ma, wait! I'm not hungry. But I do need to talk to you. Please, can't we go in the living room and just talk?" His question carried a silent apology and a desperate plea for some motherly affection. Pauline smiled and reached up and cupped Brian's cheek in her hand.

"Sure son, I'll fix us some coffee, then. Looks like you need some. Think you can rustle me up a warm fire while I start the coffee?"

"Sure, Ma - thanks."

Actually, *"rustling up a fire"* in Pauline's living room just meant turning on the gas logs, so by the time she returned, a hearty "fire" was roaring. She handed Brian a mug of coffee and sat down on the couch beside him. For several minutes they were both silent as they watched the faux flames in the fireplace flicker and dance. Never too long at a loss for words, it was Pauline who finally broke the deadening silence.

"Did you sleep with her, Brian?" she poignantly asked.

"NO, Ma! I did NOT sleep with Karla Beacham! Please, give me SOME credit!" He got up, walked over, and stood in front of the blazing fire.

"But you WERE over there, weren't you? You weren't at Rusty's meeting up with any friends, were you?" There was no use trying to hide it. Ma could always tell when he was lying.

"She sprained her ankle at work, Ma, and I just took her home. Then she asked me to stay and make her a pizza, so I did." An image flashed back to him of Karla dicing mushrooms, while he stirred the pizza sauce at the stove; a cold beer on the counter beside him. He closed his eyes, hoping to chase the regretful memory away.

"I stayed and had pizza with her, and...."

"And what, son?" Pauline questioned, afraid of her son's answer.

"She offered me a beer while we cooked. I only drank two, Ma, but you know me, –I don't drink that much anymore. I guess I had two too many...." His words trailed off and he continued to stare down at the fire, ashamed and embarrassed to look his mother in the face.

"Son, drinking isn't a sin. Unless it made you do something else." By now, Pauline could tell her son was struggling to confide a dark, painful secret in her. She knew she had to prod him firmly, but gently at the same time.

"What else happened, Brian? DID you sleep with her?" Brian finally turned and faced his mother, the fire reflecting in the tears that were now glistening in his eyes.

"No, Ma, I SWEAR on the Bible, I did NOT sleep with Karla Beacham! But..."

"But WHAT, Brian? What DID you do?" Pauline demanded. Brian slowly sat down beside Pauline and hung his head low; his shame had finally beaten him down.

"I almost did, Ma... I almost did" he softly replied. Tears splashed from his eyes onto the colorful braided hooked rug below his feet. Pauline reached over and pulled her son tightly to her chest. It was like he was nine years old again, and he had just confessed to breaking her favorite piece of Carnival glass. He always did have such a guilty conscience whenever he did something wrong. Only now, his sins were so much deeper – and more costly. Brian nestled in his mother's bosom and softly wept. This woman who had not once ounce of her blood in him, was still the only woman in the world who knew him inside and out. She brushed back his hair and patted him gently on the head.

"Take it to the Lord, son. It's nobody else's business but yours and His. We ALL go through times of temptation. Even the Good Lord was tempted by Satan. Remember what the Bible says – *"the spirit is willing, but the flesh is weak"*. God will forgive you if you ask Him. Take it to Him." Brian rose up from his mother's arms and wiped the tears from his face. She was right. He needed to spend some serious time with the Lord. About many things.

"Thanks Ma", Brian said, relieved that his secret was out in the open. He reached over and kissed her on the cheek.

"I gotta get home – got a lot of praying to do. I'll talk to you tomorrow." Pauline hugged her son once more, and then walked him to the door.

"I'll be praying too, son" she called out as he trudged back through the snowy drifts.

Safely back home, Brian piled some dry wood in the fireplace, snapped some kindling, and threw it on top. With the brisk strike of a giant kitchen match, he lit the kindling, which instantly started snapping and crackling. Before long, a warm, toasty fire was heating up the room. He sat down in his recliner and poured over the last few hours of the evening, trying to figure out where his spiritual discipline had failed him. There was plenty of blame to go around – the loneliness of the past few weeks since Emily had left; the long, physically draining hours he had spend at the tree farm; - and the alcohol that hadn't touched his lips in over ten years. But he knew deep down that the real blame was his own unfaithfulness to a wife who wasn't there, and his weak disobedience to God. Dropping to the floor on his knees, and with tears streaming down his face, he poured out his heart to a God who is only a teardrop away.

"Heavenly Father, I come to you a broken sinner. I am not worthy of the grace and forgiveness you so freely offer, but I'm asking for it anyway. I lost control tonight, and let my fleshy desires almost cause me to defile my marriage vows to Emily. More than that, I lied to Ma and made a mockery of her faith in me. I have no excuses, God – at least none that is acceptable. I sinned deeply, and I'm so ashamed of my weak actions. But I know you are a forgiving God, and I ask you now to take this burden of guilt off me, and grant me your everlasting grace, forgiveness, and peace. I have nothing to offer you in return, Father, except my promise to try harder not to fail you again. In Jesus' Name, Amen."

Broken and sorrowful, he lay on the floor in front of the fire and wept until he was drained and weary. Suddenly, he felt a light touch on his shoulder, as if someone were helping him up. Lightness settled in his heart. He knew it was the merciful hand of God lifting him up to a place of forgiveness and grace. This wonderful God who is so *rich in mercy.*

Even so, it was going to take a long time for Brian to let go of the smoldering hot coals of guilt in his soul. Not to mention, he would have to confess his wayward sin to Emily, and ask for her forgiveness as well. But after everything she had already been through losing baby Jacob, WOULD she forgive him? COULD she forgive him? It was almost too much to ask of her. But he had no choice. What if Karla Beacham spread it around town that they were together? And what if Emily somehow heard about it? She would NEVER forgive him if she found out like that! No, honesty IS the best policy, plus, he owed it to his wife to be a man and tell her what he did. If she chose NOT to forgive him, at least he was honest with her. He would expect the same from her if the situation were reversed.

He walked over to the window and glanced out. The snow had stopped falling and the full moon cast a glistening glow on the newly fallen snow below. Roy was due back at the tree farm the next day, and even though Brian was off, he decided he'd show up anyway and see if he could give Roy an extra hand. Being it was Saturday, and with the first decent snow of the season, there was sure to be lots of high-spirited Christmas tree shoppers eager to "deck the halls" with one of Beacham's famous trees! And with Karla down with her ankle, he was sure he wouldn't have to worry about running into her.

Brian turned around to make his way up to bed, and then stopped. He flipped on the porch light. For Emily. Even though he knew it was unlikely she'd show up in almost knee-deep snow, still, the light represented his ever-present faith that one day, God <u>would</u> bring her home.

Brian failed to set the alarm clock before going to bed and was still in deep slumber at ten o'clock the next morning. Had it not been for the constant banging on the front door, he might well have slept until noon. *Who could that be in this weather?* he wondered as he dragged himself down the stairs and to the front door. Opening the door, a brisk, icy wind slapped him in the face. And standing on the porch bundled up in a bright lime green Eskimo parka was Gracie, the mail lady.

"'Morning, Brian, baby! Hope I didn't wake you up! Gotta a certified letter for you here – came in last night by two-day express mail – Must be something pretty heavy! Need 'ya to sign for me, sweetie." She handed him a long, business sized envelope with a certified delivery receipt attached, along with an ink pen. *Who in the world would be sending me a certified letter? And for what?* He took the letter from Gracie's matching lime green, insulated mitten-covered hand and scribbled his name on the receipt.

"Oh, and give these treats to Babe and Pal for me, will ya? I'm kinda' running behind this morning", she said, reaching in her coat pocket and pulling out two hearty-size beefy dog treats.

"You got it, Gracie. And thanks! You be careful out there driving now!"

"No problem, Brian, baby! Me and Cher got it covered!" She tore the signature receipt off the letter, handed the letter back to Brian, and hopped back in her mail truck. As usual, the throaty caterwauling of *Cher's Greatest Hits* could be heard clean down the path as Gracie drove away.

Brian quickly retreated inside and shook the blowing snow from his hair and robe. Thankfully, the sun was already shining down strong and bright – a good start to melt the half-foot-plus of snow that had fallen the night before. And with any luck (and God's favor), a couple more days of the same would allow him to travel safely to Cherokee Hills to see Emily.

"Now, let's see who this is from", he said, walking to the kitchen to turn on the coffee pot.

He grabbed a butter knife from the drawer, sat down at the kitchen table and ripped open the envelope. *Maybe I won a sweepstakes or something; or maybe it's a certified check for some taxes I overpaid!* The adrenaline sped through his blood as he thought of all the exciting possibilities contained in the envelope he was holding. But his heart dropped, and his face turned to an ashen gray as he pulled out a document with the words *"Divorce Notice"* written in bold at the top. Through tear-blurred eyes, he read the notice aloud:

"Emily K. Clark, Petitioner/Wife vs. Brian A. Clark, Respondent/Husband. Petition for Dissolution of Marriage."

He scanned the rest of the petition as the weight of the words he read sent a cold shock of shivers up his spine. Emily was filing for divorce!

CHAPTER 15

*B*rian quickly showered and got dressed in a fog of anxiety and panic, still trying to figure how the reason for the divorce notice he had just received from Emily. He HAD to get to her – and FAST! He was not about to let her throw everything away so easily! He jumped in his truck and let it run just long enough to burn the chill off the motor. As for Brian, he was already warmed to the bone with a burning passion to find his wife and talk her out of this ridiculous divorce petition! What in the world possessed her to want to file for divorce? Or WHOM? He pulled up to Beacham's tree farm and quickly spotted Roy loading a tree for a customer. He hated to cut out on him next week, but he had to get to Cherokee Hills as soon as possible and talk to Emily.

"Hey Roy, welcome back buddy! You're already back? We sure missed you around here!" he said, giving him a friendly slap on the shoulder.

"Hey there, Brian! Yea, when we heard about the snow coming, we decided to come on back last night. It was some mighty rough traveling, but we got in about midnight! As a matter of fact, I was just getting ready to call you. Karla called me this morning and told me what happened yesterday!" Brian froze in fear of just WHAT she had told her uncle.

"About what?" Brian asked innocently.

"About her falling in the shop and spraining her ankle! She told me you took her home, too. I really appreciate you taking care of her like that! That girl is about as accident prone as her Ma was!" he laughed.

"Oh, that. Yea, well it was nothing. I mean, I was glad I was able to help her get home okay. I'm sure she'll be fine in a few days!"

"Oh sure she will. I told her to stay off that foot as much as possible. Sally's gonna go over and check on her in a little while and take her something to eat."

"Oh, so Sally came back with you?"

"Yea, she thought getting back to work might be good for her. Can't say that I wasn't happy to hear that! Especially with Karla being out for a few more days! But we should be able to handle things okay – me, Sally, you and Willie!"

"Well, that's what I came to see you about, Roy. I'm afraid I can't help you out next week. I need to make a little trip up to Cherokee Hills."

"Emily?" Roy asked.

"Yea." Brian slid his hands in his pockets and rocked back and forth on both feet."

"What is it Brian? What's wrong?" Roy asked again. Brian could hardly say the words without tearing up.

"Roy, she sent me a divorce notice! I've got to get up there right away and talk to her. I'm leaving out this afternoon."

"Oh, Brian, I'm sorry to hear that. But with the roads still covered in snow, its gonna be a tricky drive up those mountains! Why don't you wait until the plows have had time to clear them a little better? Plus, I'm sure your Ma would have a FIT if you took off up there in these conditions!"

"Well, I was kind of hoping you'd let me borrow Big Red." Big Red was Roy's fire engine red, 4x4 Dodge Ram Hemi with monster snow tires. Everyone from the local livestock vet, who was called in to deliver a baby calf in an emergency C-section, to Pastor Gray who had to perform an impromptu mountain wedding, had at one time or another borrowed Big Red for "emergency calls" when the snow made driving around Shelbyville a life-threatening event.

"Well, sure, Brian. I'd be more than happy to let you borrow Big Red. But you still need to be careful! I'm more worried about the state of your emotions more so than the state of the roads!"

"Thanks, Roy. I will. Don't worry – just send up one of those faith-filled Roy Beacham prayers for me, will ya? And one for Emily, too."

"Sure thing, Brian." Roy reached in his pocket and pulled out a big silver key with a black rubber casing on it. He tossed it over to Brian. "God speed, Brian."

*B*rian rushed back home just long enough to fill Pauline in on his plans, but decided NOT to tell her about the divorce notice. With any luck, he could talk Emily out of it and bring her back home with him. Home where she belonged. The more he thought about the craziness of it all, the more he was determined to bring her home. He was sure once she came back, they could work things out and make a fresh start. They had to. For everyone's sake. Besides, they still needed to put the memorial stone on Baby Jacob's grave. Surely, that would be the closure they both needed to put this awful tragedy behind them and start anew.

He pulled into the private drive that led to Pauline's cabin and parked the truck. *Okay, Lord, help Ma understand why I need to do this*, he prayed before he got out of the truck and walked to the door.

"Hey Ma, you here?" he called out, walking through the front door. It was agreed that after Jesse died, Brian and his Ma would have an "open door" policy to each other's houses. Just in case an emergency warranted an unannounced visit. But when Emily was there, Pauline always called first or knocked before she went in. After all, it was THEIR home, and she felt like newlyweds, of all people, needed their privacy. She, on the other hand, was always glad to see her son walk through that door.

"In here, son", Pauline called out from the kitchen. "Just putting on some venison stew for you. Figured that would taste good tonight for supper!"

"Well, I'm not gonna be here for supper tonight, Ma." Pauline turned around from the stove and gave her son a disapproving eye.

"And just exactly WHERE are you going to be?" she asked with an equally disapproving tone. Not going to make pizza again with Karla Beacham, I hope!" she teased. However, Brian was in no mood for jokes and ignored her sarcastic humor.

"I'm going to Cherokee Hills to see Emily. I've just got to see her Ma. And talk to her. I've GOT to convince her to come home NOW."

"NOW, Brian? Right after nearly a foot of snow was dumped on the roads. Why NOW? Why all the urgency?" she asked suspiciously.

"It was only five or six inches, Ma. The snow plows have nearly cleared the main roads and with the sun shining the rest of the day, even more will be melted by nightfall. Besides, it's only an hour drive and if I leave now, I may can get there and back by nightfall – and bring Emily back with me!"

Pauline searched her son's face for some kind of clue as to the REAL meaning of his sudden need to travel, but decided against interrogating him further. Things had been tense enough between them lately and the last thing she wanted was to distance her son from her even more. It was times like this she had to trust that he knew what he was doing, and had God's blessing on it, as well.

"Well, if you're that determined to go, you might ask Roy to let you borrow Big Red", she suggested.

"Already done that, Ma," he replied, holding up the big silver key to Big Red.

"Well, then, I guess you're all set." She walked over and reached up to hug him. "Be careful, son. And don't force Emily to come back if she's not ready. It will only make her that more determined to stay. Remember what Pastor Gray said – you've got to let the Lord do His work in her. And in you. It's ALL in His timing, Brian." She held him tight, and then gave him a tender kiss on the forehead.

"I'll be careful, Ma. I promise. But I really feel like God

wants me to go get my wife and bring her home. Then we can work all this other stuff out – TOGETHER." He kissed Pauline on the cheek and headed out the back door of the kitchen.

"Jesse Clark, that's ONE stubborn son you've got there!" Pauline called out in jest to her deceased husband.

Brian ran quickly back home, threw a few things in a duffel bag, then headed out on Hwy 10 toward Cherokee Hills. The bright winter sun was shining down warmly on his back as he cautiously navigated the snow-packed highway. Fortunately, traffic was light so he was able to use both lanes for most of the ride there. He popped a Christian rock CD in the CD player. Heaven's Bad Boys. He switched it to track number four – his favorite song on the CD: *In the Eye of the Storm*. He sang along to the lyrics about finding God's peace and mercy in the eye of life's storms. That's what he hoped to do by going to see Emily. Bring her back into the eye of the storm that had swallowed her up. Back to where she could find peace with Baby Jacob's death. And back where she and Brian could rekindle the God-given love they had been blessed with just a few short years before.

Nearly an hour later, Brian saw the welcome sign to Cherokee Hills, the words "WELCOME TO THE HILLS", engraved in a big stone on the side of the mountain. He had only been to Emily's mother's house once before when they were dating, but thanks to the GPS in Big Red, it carried him almost right to her doorstep. He pulled into the drive and shut off the truck. He looked around for Emily's SUV but the only vehicle there was an older model Subaru. Must be her mom's car, he figured. Hopefully, she could or WOULD tell him where to find Emily. He got out and walked to the front door, but before he had time to knock, Emily's mom had already met him on the porch.

"Brian, what are YOU doing here?" she asked in obvious surprise.

"Hello, Mrs. James. I need to see Emily. Is she here?" Barbara James stood a good six feet – almost equal to Brian's six feet two statue. Must have been where Emily got her long legs from, he guessed. She searched Brian's face with great intent. He looked as if he had aged a good fifteen years since he and Emily had married. And his eyes weren't as bright blue as she'd remembered them either. It was obvious that Emily's leaving had had a deep effect on him – both physically and emotionally. She held open the storm door and invited him inside, out of the cold.

"She's not here, Brian. But c'mon in. There's something I need to tell you about Emily. Something you need to know."

Brian followed her in, his heart beating faster in dreaded anticipation of what she was going to tell him. Had something happened to Emily? Was she in an accident or something? Had she been hurt? If so, why hadn't someone contacted him by now? Or maybe she was going to tell him that Emily had met another man, and that's why she wanted a divorce. Once again, anxious thoughts ran amok through his mind. Whatever it was Emily's mom was about to tell him, he had a sickening feeling in the pit of his stomach that it was not something he was prepared to hear. What he had hoped would be a homecoming for Emily could end up being the end, for both of them!

CHAPTER 16

"*W*hat is it, Mrs. James? What's wrong with Emily?" Brian questioned.

"Brian, didn't you get the divorce notice from the attorney?" *Divorce notice? How did SHE know about that? Unless SHE was the one that talked Emily into it?*

"Yea, I got. That's one reason I'm here. I can't believe Emily wants a divorce, Mrs. James. She's just still hurting. She needs to come home so we can work this out – she and I! I refuse to believe my wife wants to leave me!"

"Well, you better believe it, Brian. Because it's true. Emily has moved on. Don't you understand? There's nothing left for her in your world but heartache and loss. She can't live like that." Brian suddenly felt strange having such a deeply personal and sensitive conversation like this with his mother-in-law. He should be having it with his WIFE.

"No, I don't understand ANY of this! And with all due respect, Mrs. James, this is really none of your business. Don't you think this is for Emily and me to work out?"

"Brian, Emily is my daughter; and what concerns her, concerns me. I'm sure your mother feels the same way about you. Anyway, Emily doesn't WANT to see you – or TALK to you. I think she's made her intentions very clear through the divorce notice. The best thing you can do is get in your truck, turn right back around and go on back to Shelbyville, and forget about Emily. Forget about the life you had with her. Find yourself another woman and move on, Brian. Let Emily go!"

Brian was dumbfounded. He could understand Emily needing more time to grieve over losing Baby Jacob, but to just want to end it all so soon without even trying to work things out? That part he DIDN'T understand. It just didn't make any sense!

"Mrs. James, I don't know where all this is coming from, but I really need to talk to Emily! Please, tell me where I can find her! Don't you think she at least owes it to me to tell me to my face she doesn't want to be married to me anymore?"

No, Brian, I DON'T! Emily doesn't owe you ANYTHING! Now please, just leave!" She walked over, opened the front door, and showed him out. Like a whooped dog, Brian slowly retreated outside.

"And don't come back to Cherokee Hills again looking for Emily! Ever!" she ordered him as he got back in his truck.

Her cold words stung at his heart while unanswered questions spun round and round his mind. Not willing to give up so easy, he decided to try to find Emily. And he knew just where to look for her first! He quickly hurried around and down back the mountain into town. Within ten minutes, he was sitting in the parking lot of the Cherokee Hills Casino. Immediately, his thoughts rushed back to the first time he met Emily there – working in the Diamond Mine Restaurant. Maybe, just maybe she went back to work there. Maybe that's why she wasn't at her mom's house! He was hungry anyway. Might as well go in and have a bite to eat!

He jumped out of the truck and ran inside the casino. After paying twelve dollars for a meal ticket, he made his way through the crowd to the restaurant. He quickly scanned the waitresses working the tables in hopes of spotting Emily. His heart sank when he realized she was not there. A nauseous feeling settled in the pit of his stomach, crushing his appetite. Instead of going through the meal line, he graciously offered the ticket to a nearby casino player who insisted on giving him five bucks for it. He crumpled up the five dollars, shoved it in his pocket, and walked out of the casino, dejected and depressed. It seemed he had lost Emily forever.

In a desperate attempt to talk to her, he hit the speed dial number on his phone that corresponded with hers. A recording answered: *"The number you have reached has been disconnected or is no longer in service..."*. She had had her number disconnected, too. It seemed everything her mother had told him was true. It seemed Emily really DIDN'T want to be a part of Brian's life anymore! Maybe she was right – maybe he should just head back to Shelbyville and forget Emily. He bowed his head right there in his truck and said a prayer.

Father, I come to you confused and brokenhearted. I don't know what's going on with Emily, but Lord, I don't think I can take much more of this! How can I convince her to come back home if I can't even FIND her to talk to her? Please, Lord – please help me find my wife! Please help us work all this out! I know I screwed up by going over to Karla's the other night, but you've forgiven me for that and I want so badly to hold Emily in my arms again, Lord! Please give us another chance. Please bring Emily back to me!

Tears splashed down on the steering wheel as Brian opened his eyes. He turned on the ignition, looked behind him and started to back out. Suddenly, his foot hit the brake. He couldn't believe what he saw – Emily, dressed in a waitress uniform, was coming across the parking lot toward his truck! She must have just been coming in to work! He quickly put the truck in park, turned it off, jumped out, and ran to meet her as she came up behind his truck.

"Emily, thank God I found you!" he exclaimed, running up to her. Emily jumped back, startled and surprised to see Brian standing there in front of her.

"Brian, what are YOU doing here?" she asked in marked disapproval.

"Emily, we have to talk. Right here; right now!"

"Brian, I've got to get inside – my shift is about to start. Besides, I have nothing to say to you. Didn't you get the divorce notice?"

"Yes, Emily, I got it. And its crazy. I can't believe you want a divorce! Where did all THAT come from?" He tried to take her by the arms and pull her close to him but she quickly pulled away.

"No, Brian, STOP! Don't you get it? It's OVER between us! There's NOTHING to talk about! NOTHING! You're NOT going to hurt me anymore*!" Hurt her?? What did she mean by that? Her words didn't make sense.* Brian had NEVER laid a finger on her physically, and wouldn't hurt her emotionally for the world! What did she mean by he wasn't going to hurt her anymore?

"What are you talking about Emily? What have I done to hurt you? Are you blaming ME for Jacob's death? What exactly are you saying?"

"You don't KNOW? Well, why don't you go back to Shelbyville and ask your NEW GIRLFRIEND, KARLA? Maybe she can explain it to you better than I can!!! Now, please, leave me ALONE!"

Emily stormed off leaving a confused and bewildered Brian standing alone in the parking lot. Her words rang repeatedly through his head: *NEW GIRLFRIEND, KARLA… What did Emily know about Karla? HOW did she know about Karla? Emily had already left town when Karla came to Shelbyville!* The questions were becoming even more bizarre, but little by little, Brian began to piece it all together. Somehow, someway, Karla Beacham had gotten to Emily and spread a bunch of vicious lies and rumors. That HAD to be it! Pauline was right – that girl was as dangerous as a pit viper! There was no telling WHAT she had told Emily, but he was sure she was the reason Emily had filed for divorce!

Brian's blood began to boil way past the point of being healthy. He knew it was a sin to get so angry, as it says in the Psalms *–"Cease from anger, and forsake wrath: fret not thyself in any wise to do evil.* "(Psalm 37:8 KJV) But he was also only human and he hoped God could understand just WHY this news made him so mad! Luckily for Karla Beacham, it was a good hour's ride back to Shelbyville. 'Cause if he could get his hands on that girl right now, there's no telling WHAT he'd do to her! Suffice it to say, she'd be hobbling around with MORE than just a sprained ankle!

Knowing he definitely needed to calm down before he went back home, he stopped at a local coffee shop and got a cup of decaf coffee. As the warm liquid soothed his frazzled nerves, he wondered what could have made Karla Beacham deliberately sabotage his marriage. He had tried so hard to be nice to her – even forgiving her for her obvious attempts to lure him into her wicked traps. He really thought if he reached out to her that he might be able to bring her closer to God. But it was clear now she was only interested in one thing – destroying his marriage completely so she could have her way with him! Pauline and Lila Stokes were SO right about her! Why didn't he see it for himself?

Still, he needed to handle the situation in the same way Jesus would. As the young kids at church used to say, *What Would Jesus Do? Well, that's a lot easier for You than me, Lord!* Brian mused. After thinking some more about it, he decided he needed to consult with Pastor Gray, and get some spiritual counseling on the matter, BEFORE confronting Karla.

And as for Emily, once she knew the TRUTH about Karla, he was sure she'd be eager to come back home. Maybe he hadn't lost her completely just yet! Maybe what Karla had intended for his harm, God would turn into his good!

CHAPTER 17

*O*n the way back home, Brian called Pastor Gray and arranged to meet with him in his office as soon as he got back to town. He prayed fervently all the way back that the Lord would help him control his ever-growing anger and ill feelings toward Karla. When he finally arrived back in Shelbyville, he went directly over to the church. Pastor Gray warmly welcomed him in.

"Come on in and sit down, Brian. You sounded rather serious on the phone. I take it your trip to Cherokee Hills didn't go as you'd hoped?"

"Far from it, Pastor Gray. As a matter of fact, it went worse!"

"Tell me about it, son. What happened?" For the next hour and a half, Brian proceeded to tell Pastor Gray the whole ugly, sorted story about Karla – from the times she practically threw herself on him at the tree farm, to the disgraceful show of affection she so innocently schemed at her house the night before.

"But what I still can't figure out, Pastor, is how Emily found out about Karla? Karla must have talked to her at some point in time, but I don't know when or even HOW she knew how to contact her when I couldn't even find her myself!"

"Well, I'm afraid I'm to blame for that, Brian" the Pastor said.

"You see, when Karla agreed to take over the Wednesday night Bible study group, she wanted to know how the former teacher had led it, and get some suggestions from her. So I gave her Emily's cell phone number. I didn't tell her anything about you and Emily losing the baby, but I was hoping if Emily knew someone was taking over the class she used to teach, she might be persuaded to come back home. Apparently, Karla somehow found out Emily was your wife, called her up, and told her you and she were having an affair or something. I have just recently become aware of some of Karla's lies myself – such as the conniving scheme she tried to pull here at the church with you last week! She KNEW we weren't having Bible study because I called her that morning and specifically told her! And some of the other Bible study members have told me things about her too that I find quite disturbing. Of course, I do not want to judge others without having all the facts, but in light of everything that has happened I feel justified in removing her as teacher of the Bible study group. I intend to talk with her about it after church tomorrow. But in the meantime, Brian, you need to confront her yourself and let her know that you know what's been going on. As Christians, it's our duty to call our brothers and sisters out when they are disobedient to God. Not to judge or hurt them, mind you; but to encourage them to turn back to God, and support them in the arduous struggle back. You know, Brian, the Bible tells us that *ALL have sinned and fallen short of God's glory.* And even though no one would fault you for being angry with Karla, it is more important for you to forgive her and pray for her. Just as Christ has done for us all."

Even though it was not exactly what Brian wanted to hear, he knew Pastor Gray was right. Harboring anger and hate in his heart for Karla was not only going to fester and grow inside his heart, but it was clearly disobedient to what God instructs us to do in His Word. Brian was glad he came to see Pastor Gray first, but now he knew he needed to set things straight with Karla. Not in a mean, hurtful way, but a loving, Christ-like way.

"Thanks, Pastor. You've been a big help. Please pray for me and Emily. I want so badly for her to come home by Christmas."

"My thoughts and prayers are with you and Emily constantly, Brian. Put it in God's hands, then let it go. He'll work it out in His own time, and in His own way. Don't worry – He's NOT going to end this on a negative note!" Pastor Gray's words were uplifting and encouraging, and Brian felt a new sense of peace and hope for his future with Emily.

After he left the church, Brian drove directly over to Karla's house. Her Corvette was parked in the yard. Roy and Sally must have taken it back over to her when they returned home. With confidence in God's guidance, and Pastor Gray's wise counsel, Brian walked up to the door and firmly knocked. A few moments later, Karla appeared in a pair of black sweat pants and a red pullover sweater. As usual, the sweater revealed more than it covered, and she was poured into the sweat pants like a bottle of thick syrup. *What a shame that such an attractive girl displays such unattractive behavior,* Brian thought.

"Brian, hey, what are you doing here?" Karla meekly asked.

"Hi Karla. I'm sorry to come over without calling first, but I really need to talk to you. Can I come in for a few minutes?" Despite his still burning anger toward her, his tone was polite and respectful. She looked at him with a puzzled, yet pleased expression.

"Sure, come in. I'm glad you came over. I've been feeling kind of lonely today."

"How's your ankle?" Brian asked.

"Oh, it's much better. I'm not hobbling around nearly as much, and the pain has all but gone. By the way, I don't think I thanked you properly for bringing me home last night." She reached over and tried to kiss Brian on the lips, but he firmly pushed her away.

"No, Karla, STOP! Listen to me, you have got to STOP coming onto me! I'm a happily married man and I am NOT interested in being with anyone but Emily! I know you've been talking to her, and telling her lies about me and you and its got to STOP NOW! Do you understand? You've got to STOP lying and manipulating people to get your way? It's wrong, Karla – don't you know that? I thought you said you were a Christian! How can you deliberately go against God's Word?" Karla looked up at Brian in utter shock and surprise. Her secrets were out and now she risked losing him forever! She began to softly cry and tried to hide her face in Brian's chest. Once again, he pushed her away.

"Karla, stop. It's not going to work. You need help, Karla. You're hurting over something inside and you need someone to help you sort it all out so you'll feel better! I can get you some help, Karla. Pastor Gray knows several really good therapists that can help you. Let me call him for you and arrange for you to meet with someone. I'll even take you there myself. Please, do it for yourself, Karla. I promise you'll be a much happier person if you'll just get some help." Karla pulled back from Brian and walked slowly toward the kitchen.

"You're right, Brian – I DO need some help" she deliberately agreed. "But I can make the call myself. Just let me get something to write the number down with."

Brian followed her to the kitchen, relieved she was agreeing to get finally get help. Karla reached into her purse that was on the counter, as if she were looking for a pen, but pulled out a .38 revolver instead. She quickly spun around and pointed the gun directly at Brian.

"Liar! You don't care about me! All you want is to get rid of me so you can be with HER!" she screamed as she circled round and round him, pointing the gun at his chest.

"I have tried my BEST to be good to you but you keep running back to her – talking about Emily. Emily this, and Emily that – I'm SO SICK of hearing about poor Emily!! What about ME, Brian? When are you going to pay some attention to ME?"

Brian slowly backed away, retreating into the living room, and prayed to God to send every available angel to his side. He knew Karla had some emotional issues, but he never dreamed she'd take things THIS far! She followed him into the living room, keeping the gun pointed directly to his chest.

"Karla, calm down. It's not all that bad. Let's talk some more about this. I told you – I can get you some help and one day you WILL find a man who wants to be with you. But that man can't be ME, Karla. I'm already committed to someone else. Don't you understand that? You can't have me, Karla!"

"Shut up, Brian! I don't want to hear anymore of your lies! I'LL decide who I want and DON'T want in my life! NOT YOU, or Pastor Gray, or ANYONE ELSE!" She put the revolver to her lips and seductively licked the barrel tip.

"You know, it's a good thing it snowed so much last night, 'cause I was gonna take a little trip today myself, Brian! Wanna know where I was going?" She laughed a vile little laugh.

"I was going up to Cherokee Hills, too! I wanted to go see poor Emily. I've been SO worried about her since she left – just like you, Brian! I thought I might go "put her out of her misery", so to speak!" She laughed another sickening laugh, and then pointed the gun again at Brian.

"But maybe I'll put YOU out of MY misery first!" she heckled. He inched backwards, closer to the door but she ordered him to move away and sit down on the couch. The situation was as tense as a nun showing up in a strip club, and Brian was sure God was sleeping on the job. However, this was no joking matter. Karla could snap at any moment. He prayed for the quick and decisive wisdom of old King Solomon. Right on cue, God sent an answer. Brian hung his head down as if in despair, and choked up a few crocodile tears himself.

"Karla, you're right. I have been going on way too much about Emily. And I have to be honest with you. Emily and I are getting a divorce. She doesn't want to be married to me anymore. I lied to you earlier because I was hurt and confused. I wasn't sure you'd still want me. I hope you can forgive me. " He buried his head in his hands, peeking through his fingers to keep an eye on Karla. Falling now for his act, she immediately rushed over to console him, throwing the revolver down beside him on the couch.

"Oh, Brian, baby, it's okay, I'm here. I'll take care of you. You don't need Emily – it's me you want! I'm the one you really love, right?" She swooned over him, kissing him repeatedly on his face and lips. While Karla was caught up in the moment, and knowing he only had a tiny window of opportunity, he quickly reached down, grabbed the gun, and pushed Karla away.

"It's over Karla – get back!" he ordered. Karla started to sob and begged him to hold her. He pushed her back and she fell to the floor.

"Stay there, Karla. Don't get up. I'm calling the police." With the gun still pointed at her, he dialed 911 on his cell phone and hit the speakerphone button.

"This is 911 – What is your emergency?"

"Yea, I have a woman here who tried to kill me, but I managed to get her gun and I've got it on her now. Please send someone A.S.A.P to 113 Hawks Nest Trail. And hurry!

"Okay, sir, stay on the line with me while I dispatch an officer. Are you okay, and is the woman okay?"

As Brian continued to talk with the operator, Karla curled up in a fetal position and continued to sob. Brian's heart reached out to her in a way that surprised him. For the first time, he didn't see a manipulative, scheming, deceptive woman. All he could see was a scared, frightened little girl who only wanted to be loved. He didn't know what had happened to her in her life to leave such deep emotional scars, but at that moment, all he could feel for her was the love of Christ. While waiting for the police to come, he sent up a silent prayer for Karla Beacham.

Father, wrap your loving arms around this woman and comfort her. Help her to find her way back to You, and get the emotional, mental, and spiritual help she needs. Amen.

It was then Brian realized why God had allowed their paths to cross. Who knows what Karla may have done if she'd continued on the same wicked path? At least now, she could get some help –even if it was within the confines of a prison cell.

Within minutes, the police arrived, and took Karla Beacham into custody. Brian called Roy and Pastor Gray and told them what happened, and after Pastor Gray picked up Roy, they met Brian at the police station.

"I'm so sorry, Roy – I really tried to help Karla, but she needs professional help" Brian said upon Roy's arrival.

"She has for many years, Brian – I'm just grateful to God she didn't hurt anyone. And I'm glad her parents aren't around to see what's become of her."

"I'll keep you all in my prayers" Brian replied.

"Thanks, son – for everything..."

While Roy stayed and talked with the police about Karla, Pastor Gray took Brian home to a worried and waiting Pauline.

"Thank God you're alright, son! I KNEW that woman was trouble – didn't I tell you??" Pauline scolded, the whole time she was hugging her son.

"Ma, Karla needs help. She's got some serious emotional problems. We should be praying for her – not judging her, remember?"

"I will pray for her, son, but she's also a DANGEROUS woman, and you could have been killed! Not to mention Emily! Thank God for that snow storm yesterday, otherwise, that crazy woman might have gone to Cherokee Hills and hunted your wife down and killed her, too!"

"I know, Ma, but it's all over now. At least that part. I've still got a lot of things to explain to Emily. I just hope she and her mother will give me a chance to do that. Pastor Gray has offered to go back up there with me tomorrow afternoon to see them. I sure could use some support from my Ma, too!" He winked and cast Pauline a bashful smile.

"Are you kidding, son? Of course I'm going up there with you and the Pastor! I wouldn't DREAM of letting you go back up there without me!" she replied matter-of-factly.

In spite of the harrowing day's events, Brian slept like a baby that night. He rested well knowing that within a few short hours, he would be back in Cherokee Hills, and this time, he WOULD bring Emily back home!

CHAPTER 18

*D*irectly after church the next day, Brian, Pauline, and Pastor Gray left for Cherokee Hills. The roads were much more passable, thanks to an all night snow plow crew, and the melting rays of another unusually warm and sunny December sun. Soon, they were rounding the curve into Cherokee Hills, and just a short distance from Emily's mom's house. This time, Emily's mom's car was gone, but Emily's SUV was parked in the drive. She was there. And hopefully alone. Pauline said a quick prayer for Brian, who at the same time, was saying one for Emily. Pastor Gray was praying for them all.

"Maybe I better go in first," Pastor Gray suggested. "She might be more willing to talk to me since I'm sort of an impartial party."

"Sounds like a plan", Brian replied. Pastor Gray stepped out of the truck, walked up to the front door, and tapped on it lightly. Within seconds, Emily appeared in the doorway.

"Hello Emily", Pastor Gray said.

"Pastor Gray – what are you doing here?" she asked.

"Well, first of all, you should know I'm not alone." He pointed to the truck where Brian and Pauline were waiting. Emily peered around him and squinted through the blaring sun to see who he was referring to. Then she spotted Brian and Pauline. She started to shut the door on Pastor Gray, but he held it open with his arm.

"Wait, Emily, please. Let me come in and talk with you for a minute. This is so important. There are some things you don't know – things you need to be aware of. Brian hasn't betrayed you like you think – you've got to hear the truth!"

Reluctantly, Emily invited him in, but quickly slammed

the door behind him, lest Pauline and Brian should try to come in, too.

"What is this all about, Pastor Gray?" Emily demanded.

"Are we alone Emily? Is you mother here?"

"No, she's out shopping. What's going on, Pastor Gray? Why did you bring Brian and his mother up here? I told him I didn't want to see him again. Didn't he tell you about the divorce notice?"

"Yes, Emily, he did. But you've got it all wrong. Brian has NOT been unfaithful to you! As a matter of fact, he's just been through a very difficult and tense situation with Karla Beacham, and...." Emily interrupted him before he could continue.

"HE'S been through a difficult situation? What about ME? I'M the one he had an affair on! I'M the one he cheated on! You've got a lot of nerve coming here to defend HIM!!"

"Emily, WAIT! That's NOT TRUE! If you'll just listen a minute, I'll explain it!" Emily folded her arms defiantly in front of her chest and turned her back to him.

"Please, Emily, can't we sit down on the sofa and talk for a minute? You've got it all wrong!" Finally, Emily agreed and quietly sat down. Pastor Gray sat down beside her.

"Karla Beacham is in jail, Emily. She was arrested last night for attempted murder." Emily looked up at Pastor Gray in surprise.

"Who did she try to kill?" she asked.

"Brian. She tried to kill your husband, Emily." Emily gasped in shock.

"What happened, Pastor? Is Brian alright?"

"Yes, he's fine. He had gone to her house to try to talk to her and let her know he knew she was the one that had lied to you about their "so-called affair". She got upset with him, and pulled a gun out of her purse and threatened him with it. It was a close call, Emily, but Brian was able to get the gun away from her and call the police. They took her away to the State Penitentiary. It was a very dangerous situation, but God protected Brian.

"Oh my God, I had no idea" Emily replied, her defenses lowering.

"Everything she told you was a lie, Emily. Brian and Karla were absolutely NOT having an affair. She was obsessed with him and wanted him so badly that she lied to you to try and break up your marriage. She's an evil and wicked woman with a lot of emotional problems to deal with. Brian was just being nice to her and she made it into something lewd and dishonest. You HAVE to believe me Emily – as a man of God, I hope you know I wouldn't make all this up, or defend a man who was guilty of fornication." Emily got up and walked to the window. She peeped out the curtains and saw Brian still sitting in the car.

"Please, Emily, just talk to him. Give him a chance. He's been so hurt since you left – all he really wants is his wife. And in the eyes of God, you are STILL his wife. You owe it to him to talk to him, Emily. And you owe it to God to honor your marriage vows by trying to work this out with your husband – together. Shall I go out and get him?" Emily nodded her head "yes". Pastor Gray went outside and instructed Brian that it was all right to go in.

"Pauline and I will go into town to the coffee shop while you and Emily talk. Call us when you're ready to leave." He patted Brian on the shoulder.

"Be gentle with her, Brian – she's still hurting". Brian nodded and went up to the door. Emily met him there and showed him in, as Pastor Gray and Pauline headed into town.

"Hello, Emily. Thanks for agreeing to see me. I can only imagine what must be going through your mind. Did Pastor Gray tell you what happened last night?" Emily nodded but didn't speak. Brian laid his finger on her chin and gently persuaded her to look up into his eyes.

"Look, Emily, I don't have all the answers, but I do know that we can't work anything out if we're in two separate places. I'm sorry I can't grieve over Jacob the way you think I should grieve. But make no mistake – I AM grieving." He took her hands tightly in his. There were big tears in his eyes as he continued speaking.

"For God's sake, Emily, he was MY SON, TOO! The son I always wanted! It was like someone kicked me in the gut when he died! I may not show my pain like you do, but believe me – it hurts like HELL!" He stood there holding her hands tightly, both their tears splashing down on them.

Emily looked up at her husband and for the first time in weeks, her icy heart started to melt away. As she stared into his eyes, his tears became hers. She fell forward into his arms and sobbed uncontrollably. Brian pulled his wife in closer to him and held her tightly against his chest, feeling the hurt, and pain drain from her body. For what seemed like hours, they just stood there, holding each other; crying, and mourning the loss of not only baby Jacob, but of the time they had let so carelessly slip by without each other.

Finally, Emily pulled back. Brian took her face once again in his hands and gently reached down and kissed her. As her soft, velvety lips melted into his, a spark of passion was re-ignited inside both their hearts and souls. The love that God had blessed them with just a few years earlier was still there – despite all the tragedy, heartache and deception that had tried to steal it away. As their kiss came to its end, Brian pulled Emily back into a warm embrace and held her tightly a few minutes longer

"Ready to come home now?" he whispered in her ear.

She looked up at him, smiled and whispered back faintly, *"yes"*.

"Need help packing?" he asked.

"No, I don't have that much. I'll be ready in a few minutes." Brian released her so she could go pack, and then called Pauline.

"Ma, it's me. You and Pastor Gray can head on back to Shelbyville. Emily and I will be coming behind you shortly.

"Emily? Emily's coming back with you?"

"Yes, Ma. Emily's coming home, too! We're driving her car back to Shelbyville. I told you, Ma – I told you one day Emily WOULD come home!"

"Yes, you did, son. You certainly did. Praise God!"

Even though the ride home from Cherokee Hills was somewhat silent and awkward, Brian and Emily managed to keep the conversation going without getting into a lot of heavy talk. Brian knew they still had a lot to work out, but at least now that Emily was coming home, they could work it out TOGETHER.

He thought again about the memorial stone for baby Jacob. It was still in the crate on the front porch, and he had yet to mention it to Emily. Maybe that would be the perfect starting point for Emily to start letting go of the pain and loss that almost destroyed them. Yes, that needed to be taken care of first!

CHAPTER 19

*P*astor Gray dropped Pauline off at Brian and Emily's house, and then headed home himself.

"I'll be praying for you, all," he replied as Pauline exited the truck.

"Thanks, Pastor. For everything. Shelbyville is blessed to have you as our Pastor!" Pauline said.

"Thanks, Pauline. But give credit where credit is due", he replied, pointing up to the heavens above him. Pauline smiled back and nodded. God certainly deserved the credit for this one! It wasn't long before Brian and Emily arrived, and Pauline excitedly hurried out to welcome Emily home.

"It's good to finally have you home, Emily, she exclaimed, holding out her arms in a welcoming embrace. You let me know if there's anything I can do, okay?" she whispered in her daughter-in-law's ear.

"Thanks, Pauline. I will" Emily tearfully nodded back. Pauline looked over at Brian and winked. He winked back, as if to say, "told you so!" Still, Pauline prayed that her son and daughter in law could move on from the harrowing experiences of the past few months. Knowing they had a lot to discuss, Pauline went back home and left Brian and Emily alone. As Brian ushered Emily up to the steps, she stopped when she saw the crate.

"What's that?" she asked.

"It's Jacob's memorial stone. It arrived last week. I've been waiting until you got home, so we could put it up together." Emily just stood there – almost like she was frozen in time. Brian quickly prodded her inside, out of the cold, and away from the painful memories that were staring back at her from the wooden crate.

Once inside, Brian started a fire while Emily rested on the couch. As the glowing embers erupted into a blazing fire, he joined her on the couch. They stared at the fire for several minutes – neither one speaking a word. Brian really didn't know where to start. He had waited so long for this moment, and now that Emily was home, he had no clue what to do or say to move forward.

Finally, he heard a voice speak to his spirit: *Dance with her.* Dance with her? He wondered if his mind was playing tricks on him. The voice spoke to him again: *Dance with your wife, Brian. Like you used to.* Slowly, he got up, went over to the stereo and turned on some light music. He turned back around to Emily and held out his hand, coaxing her up from the couch. She took his hand and he pulled her close to him, then begin to slow dance with her around the room. They danced spiritedly for several minutes – Brian holding her close one minute, then spinning her gracefully around the next. They danced like they used to when they first married. They danced around the living room, through the hall and into the kitchen. Before long, Emily was smiling and laughing - waltzing around as carefree as a butterfly. Brian, too, showed off his two-step and even pulled off a very good disco move, to which Emily burst into uncontrollable laughter. As the music continued to play through the whole house speaker system, Brian and Emily danced to every song. Finally, exhausted and drained, they collapsed on the couch in the living room.

As they caught their breaths, Brian reached over and once again passionately kissed his wife. She longingly kissed him back. It had been so long for them both. Brian got up, then picked Emily up and toted her upstairs to their bedroom. Her thin, lanky body went limp in his strong, Herculean hold, and she felt like a princess as he carried her up. As he laid her gently on the bed, the air in the room was filled with unbridled passion and unfulfilled desire. For so many weeks, Brian had dreamed of this moment. The moment he could finally make love to his wife again. As he pulled back the covers and crawled in bed beside her, he could hardly contain the love she eagerly awaited for. For hours, they made love. Pure, perfect, virtuous love. And when they were done, time stood still as they caressed and held each other in their arms til they drifted peacefully off to sleep, holding each other tightly throughout the night.

*B*rian awoke first the next morning and looked over at Emily who was still nestled deeply in his arms. He closed his eyes and thanked God not only for a new day, but for finally bringing Emily back home. He reached over and kissed her gently on the forehead while she slept. Then, letting her sleep, he quietly slipped out of bed to go downstairs and fix breakfast.

Soon, the aroma of fresh deer sausage with sage, and cinnamon streusel rolls wakened Emily from her sleep. Throwing on a robe, she wandered downstairs to find Brian whistling happily in the kitchen, greeting her with a fresh cup of hot French vanilla coffee as she came in the kitchen.

"Wow, it smells wonderful in here! I'd forgotten what a wonderful breakfast you make!" she said.

"Well, allow me to refresh your memory" Brian replied, holding a gooey cinnamon roll up to her lips. She took a bite from one end while Brian bit the other, then he licked the icing from her lips, ending in a sweet, sticky kiss. It felt so good to have Emily back in the house again. She brought so much life to everything. Brian had so missed that.

They shared another cinnamon roll and some deer sausage, and talked about Brian's job at the tree farm, while they ate. He had called Roy earlier and told him that Emily had come home, to which Roy insisted he take a few more days off to spend with her. They had so much catching up to do, but Brian decided to take things slow and easy. They both needed time to readjust to each other, not to mention time to move forward without the dark, painful cloud of memories of losing baby Jacob hanging over their heads. He knew he had to take things at Emily's pace and just be patient with her. When the time was right he would talk to her about getting some counseling to help them work through everything. But right now, they just needed to be with each other and rediscover the love God had given them.

"I want to go see Jacob's grave," Emily boldly announced, unexpectedly. "And I want us to put up the memorial stone together." She smiled at Brian through teary eyes. He smiled back at his beautiful wife.

"I'd like that. Do you want to go today?" he asked.

"Yes, the sooner, the better. I'll go upstairs and get dressed. Will you load the stone in the truck?" Brian walked around and put his arms around her. She leaned her head on his shoulder.

"You go on up. I'll be ready when you are" he replied.

Emily went upstairs and got dressed while Brian cleaned up the kitchen, then went outside and loaded the crate with the memorial stone, on the truck. A few minutes later, Emily appeared on the porch, clutching a picture of baby Jacob to put in the picture frame of the memorial stone.

A gray and threatening snow cloud followed them as they drove the five miles out to the Shelbyville Memorial Gardens, where baby Jacob was laid to rest. The skies were overcast and cloudy, and a few snow flurries misted the air as they got out of the truck. Brian lifted the stone from the crate and toted it while Emily held onto his arm for support. When they reached Jacob's grave, Brian placed the memorial stone in its stand and placed it at the foot of his grave. Emily carefully inserted the picture in the frame, being careful to make sure the acrylic protector was securely in place. Then she kissed her fingers and placed them on his picture. A tear slipped from her eye and fell on the grave.

Together, they knelt down in front of baby Jacob's grave and wept; Emily sobbing softly in Brian's chest. With tears streaming down his face, Brian lifted his face to Heaven and said a prayer:

"Father, take good care of our son. And tell him we love him and miss him. And God, help us to let go of Jacob, just as You had to let go of Your Son. For we know, just like You, one day we will see OUR son again, too! Amen."

"Amen", Emily repeated through muffled sobs. Brian lifted Emily up, her knees weak and wobbly with grief. She leaned on him once more for support, as they slowly walked back to the truck. Suddenly, the sun burst forth from the cloudy skies and shone down brightly on baby Jacob's grave. Both Brian and Emily looked up at the sun as it got brighter and brighter. They knew then that baby Jacob was safe and warm in the arms of Jesus, waiting patiently for the day when they would join him. Emily smiled at Brian. Her smile said it all. She had finally let go of baby Jacob, and finally come home! Just like he ALWAYS knew she would!

THE END

"At that time I will gather you;
at that time I will bring you home."
– Zephaniah 3:20 NIV

If you enjoyed reading
Letting Go: Emily's Homecoming,
send the author an email with your comments:

Lisa A. Tippette
ltippette@yahoo.com

Other books by Lisa A. Tippette:
-*Broken Dreams and Answered Prayers* (2012)

Thank you for supporting Independent Authors!

Made in the USA
Charleston, SC
02 December 2013